Totally Bound Publishing books by CC Dragon

Southern Belle Cozy Mysteries
The Mint Julep Murder
The Heavenly Hazelnut Murder

I0670565

Southern Belle Cozy Mysteries

THE HEAVENLY HAZELNUT MURDER

CC DRAGON

The Heavenly Hazelnut Murder
ISBN # 978-1-83943-936-0
©Copyright CC Dragon 2021
Cover Art by Louisa Maggio ©Copyright January 2021
Interior text design by Claire Siemaszkiewicz
Totally Bound Publishing

Published in 2021 by Totally Bound Publishing, United Kingdom.

THE HEAVENLY HAZELNUT MURDER

Chapter One

"Harry!" I shouted across the back of the Honey Buckle bar. "Keg change now, please!"

One of Katie's brothers gave me a thumbs up and went to the back.

"Busy?" Lurlene teased as she nursed a margarita.

"As a one-legged man in a butt-kicking contest, thanks for your concern," I replied to my old high school nemesis. She and I had an uneasy truce, or she was being fake-nice. Sometimes it was hard to tell. In the south, people were nice when they were insulting a person to their face.

She smiled and glanced at my hands as I set down fresh coasters. "I could fix up your nails. A nice French tip or something. Clean but to actually show you're a lady."

"Thanks, but I do too much baking with Gran. I can't risk any chips coming off in the dough," I replied.

"Wear gloves. That's how real places prep food. Yuck," Lurlene said.

"Everything we do is homemade to the highest standards. Gran is a clean freak and you know it. But gloves are a good idea," I admitted. "We use them at the shop, of course, but a lot is made at home."

Katie sighed. "This is cute, you two actually talking nice for a minute, and we're all happy you started cosmetology school, Lurlene, but Belle has customers. She's here to work. Get yourself a life."

Lurlene glared at Katie. That wasn't normal for Katie at all. She got firm when needed with people who overindulged, but she'd never snap at paying customers. Maybe I was just off today?

"Sorry, it's hard to be nice to customers and be efficient. We were cackling like hens. Where's Martha?" I asked Katie. I had a degree in hospitality but the small town south had its own rules about being nice. I missed the city for the anonymity and the money. Still, Gran had had a few spells and needed someone around. My parents had run off after I was born, and my grandfather was dead, so it was down to me. I'd never minded being an only child before and I loved Gran to bits, but it'd be nice to have someone to share the pressure with — to run options with. But no, there was just me.

Martha, another friend from high school, was working tonight too. Katie pointed to the tables of thirsty patrons and I caught a glimpse of Martha in the crowd. "She's got the tables now. You've got new guys at the bar. Keep 'em coming."

I turned and smiled at the new guys. "What's your poison?"

"Four beers," one ordered.

I popped open four bottles of beer.

"We wanted tap," he said, like I was an idiot.

I grinned. "People in hell want ice water. Keg is dead. I'm waiting for a change. You want it now? Then you get the bottle. Next round will be tap."

They grumbled, but I kept a smile plastered on my face. More complaining and they might get around half off, but I wasn't giving it away because we were busy.

Martha walked up with a tray of empties. "Sorry, my ex called twice. Like he can't watch his own kids for one night."

Harry carried out a keg. "Make way, ladies. I'm here to rescue the bar."

"How helpful." Martha blushed.

"You could've checked the kegs before opening and been a real knight in shining armor," I scolded.

"Have you met my sister? We're going to waste the last five glasses in one keg because it's *close* to change? That's not how you make money," Harry warned.

Katie poked me in the arm. "He's right. Let him work, and you hit the blender. Girls' night in the corner and they want another round of margaritas."

"On it. Strawberry again?" I enjoyed the blended drinks. It felt like making smoothies at my own shop.

"Yep, then we'll be out of strawberries, but they won't care. If they want another round, switch them out to lime." Katie waved it off and her many bangles jingled.

She looked like she should be running a bar. Always dressed like a cowgirl, Katie wore a tight T-shirt that promoted her establishment. Big jewelry and a big smile were part of her ensemble. Her family was a mishmash of a train wreck, like mine, so we'd been besties forever.

While Katie filled Martha's orders for the tables, I blended up a bunch of frozen cocktails. Harry set up the keg and drew himself one.

I shot him a look. "Saw that. Not when you're working."

"Gotta test my work for quality." He grinned. "It's mostly foam, it's for the customers. They'll get a good pull."

"Working okay?" I teased.

He nodded.

"Great. I think we're stocked now up here, so take those dirty glasses with you to the back. Run a load of glasses, then we might need you bouncing. People seem to want a keg attached to their mouths."

"You're as bossy as my sister," he said.

"I'm happy to run the dishwasher if you want to tend bar. Bouncing, that's not me. I'm a tiny blonde. They'd just laugh at me." I checked my image in the mirror behind the bar. My ponytail was still high and tight. Makeup was fine. I wore a Honey Buckle T-shirt, jeans and gym shoes with good support. What? No one saw my feet behind the bar. When I went out, I could rock heels like any good southern girl, but the right shoes for the right job…

"Fine. I don't like dealing with people. I got a new job anyway. Day job," Harry said.

"Congrats. But your sister needs you now and that's what family is for." I nudged the tray of empty glasses at him to clear.

He did and disappeared in the back.

I loaded the margaritas up on a fresh tray as Martha picked up another one ready for her tables. "He's so nice," Martha said.

"Harry? Yeah, a prince. He'll want a hug for running the dishwasher. Need me to take these?" I asked.

"I'll do it. You spill," Katie cut in.

It was true. I'm not the best with a tray. When I tried to waitress once, I failed miserably and ended up working in coffee shops. "I slung coffee at Starbucks for years, but those cups generally had lids. Why does coffee always have a lid and alcohol so rarely does? Seems like people drinking booze would spill more," I pondered.

Katie chuckled. "They spill it, they want more, so they'll just buy more. Better for business not to have lids. Coffee people would just demand a free refill."

"You really did find the perfect business to run," I teased my best friend.

"Thanks. Gotta go introduce the band. Gus is sitting with them sometime tonight...hope that's okay," Katie said.

"Sure. I've been dating Luke for a few weeks. Gus is old news," I said. Gus was the local sheriff who'd been flirting with me since he moved into town. Unfortunately, his past was more complicated than he'd let on. Everyone had a past, but if a man doesn't 'fess up and the other woman still has the ring, it's just too much drama for me. Even if the man was tall, handsome, musical and seemed good at heart.

Katie arched an eyebrow but headed off. As the band played, without Gus as of yet, the crowd calmed down to nurse their beverages instead of downing them like they were dying of thirst.

Martha and Katie made it to the bar and we restocked a bit before enjoying the music.

"What happened with Gus?" Martha asked.

"Nothing, I told you...we were solving a murder together. We also happened to run into his ex-fiancée at a dive bar. She gave him the ring back. Very weird. But I'm not looking for that sort of drama or a guy that fresh off of a super-serious relationship," I said.

"You and Pastor Luke are a couple now? Rebound maybe, but it'll never work," Lurlene snarked.

11

"Oh, goodie, are we back to the mean girls thing?" I teased.

Lurlene shook her head. "I'm being nice here. See, people always think I'm being mean when I'm trying to be constructively kind and give them a heads-up on the rest of the world. How people really think. You're too sweet and Katie is too polite to tell you, but the pastor isn't going to get serious about someone with your history. Your past—it's not your fault but it's not a secret."

"That's a pretty crappy pastor," Martha remarked then waved back at a table signaling her. "I'm going to make a round."

"Thanks, Martha. Lurlene, quit it," Katie warned.

"No, go on. A pastor is going to judge me for my parents running off after I was born and leaving me with Gran? They were young and clearly not ready to be parents. That's not my fault. I was raised right by my grandparents," I defended myself.

"That is all true. You even try extra hard to be a Goody Two-shoes, and he's not going to judge you for their behavior...he's going to judge you for yours. Running off to the big city alone," she pointed out.

"Otherwise known as going to college," I replied.

"Not all colleges are big-city ones. Plus you're working in a bar. You're simply not pastor's wife material," she said.

"We're just dating! I'm not looking for a husband! Hey, has anyone seen Big Ed? I know I don't work every night, but he was a regular and he's been gone awhile."

"He's a long-haul trucker. He'll be gone a week or so at a time. Then he's home for a week or just a weekend. Give it a week or so and he'll turn up—he always does." Katie waved it off.

"Nice trying to dodge the topic. You'd be better off with a guy like Gus." Lurlene winked.

Just then, Gus sat at the bar. "Are my ears burning?'

"Katie mentioned you'd be sitting in with the band. Guess you're late," I replied.

"Sitting in doesn't mean their whole set. What's this I hear about your grandmother letting the musicians park on her land?" he asked.

I lifted a shoulder. "She's nice to people. They needed a place to park and I guess the trailer lots around town were full. That or the guys made too much noise."

"Very charitable of her. Any trouble, you call me." Luke appeared through the crowd like he'd been lurking and listening.

I did my best to mask my surprise. He sat on the other side of Lurlene and another guy sat next him. There was enough of a resemblance between them that I knew he had to be a cousin or some relation.

"Hey, what can I get you two?" I asked.

"Musicians can be a little wild and rough around the edges, if you need any help," Gus offered.

"Got it. Thanks! Nine-one-one is easy to remember." I smiled.

Just then the band noticed Gus and called him up. I breathed a sigh of relief and focused on Luke.

"Busy night," he said.

"Yep, otherwise they wouldn't need me and Martha. Who's your friend?" I asked.

"Sorry—I'm Pete, Lucas' little brother. He's not a fan." The guy introduced himself.

"He's never mentioned you." I frowned and glanced at Lucas. "Welcome to the Honey Buckle! What would you like to drink?"

"Just whatever's on tap," he replied.

13

"Luke?" I offered.

"Just a water," he said.

"No problem." I filled the order and set the drinks down. "Everything okay?"

"We need to speak privately." He looked around.

"Kind of busy right now," I countered.

Martha walked up with an order and I filled it.

"Pastor." One of Katie's brothers rushed up. "Can we talk?"

Luke looked from me to his brother to Larry. "I guess."

"It's your job to talk to your flock whenever they need you. Go for it," Pete said.

I nodded as Katie walked up with another order. "I'm busy here."

Luke took his water and slipped away from the bar.

"I'm the fun one," Pete informed.

"Luke can be fun."

Pete grinned. "I hope you don't mind I'll be crashing with my brother for a few days. He's not one for visiting home much. But I don't want to be in your way."

"My way? I'm not that fast or easy. We've only been dating a couple of weeks," I said.

"A good girl who is really good. Yet you work in a bar," he teased.

I held up one finger while I blasted the blender for the new batch of margaritas then went about pouring them. "I am a good girl. My best friend owns this bar, so I'll be hanging out here or helping her out whenever she needs it. I like the music and I'm over twenty-one, so it's really nobody's business," I replied.

Pete sighed. "Everything is everyone's business in a small town. If this isn't your job, what is?"

"My grandmother and I own a shop in town. Pastries and jam to go with them, plus fancy coffee and smoothies. Your brother's favorite is Heavenly Hazelnut. He actually helped to name it."

"Sounds about right. No caffeine or alcohol. He goes to extremes."

I wanted to ask more about that, but Lurlene swooped in. Pete was younger and even a bit more handsome than his brother.

"How do you do?" Lurlene blushed. "I'm so sorry. We haven't been introduced. Annabelle Baxter, you have just the worst manners. I'm Lurlene. I'm in beauty school and I work at my daddy's store."

"Lurlene, this is Pastor Luke's younger brother, Pete." I fulfilled my obligation to introduce and inform.

He shook her hand. "I don't know why you're in school—you look like you've got that beauty thing nailed down perfect."

"You flatterer. Now answer my question. What's the younger brother of a preacher do to make his mama proud?" she asked.

I wanted to down one of those margaritas as I lifted the tray slowly.

"I'm a paramedic and fireman. I worked for my hometown and I'm thinking of maybe moving. You guys have a county system here because things are so spread out, but it'd be a different sort of a challenge," he said.

"Nice to be near your brother. So sweet," she replied.

I carried the tray carefully, dodging dancing couples and patrons who felt no pain. Many would be praying to the porcelain god tonight. I caught Luke's eye as he chatted with Larry in the corner. Why did I feel so bad? I hadn't done a thing but help my friend. Our church wasn't one of those super-strict, no drinking, no dancing groups — a good solid Christian church was all. I held my head up high and steadied the tray, but someone had spilled on the edge of the dancefloor as I neared the stage.

Gus hopped down. "Let go." I released my grip on the drinks but fell flat on my backside.

The whole place erupted in applause, laughs and whistles. Martha rushed over and helped me up. Then she took the tray from Gus and delivered the drinks. My face felt like I'd suffered a facial treatment in hell, it burned so hot. I took the bar towel I'd had slung over my shoulder and wiped up the spill.

"You okay?" Gus asked.

"Fine. Thanks for saving the drinks." I headed back to the bar.

Gus followed. "I'd have grabbed you, but then you'd have been wearing all those drinks and I'd be holding you up. Don't think your boyfriend would like that. I couldn't save you both and I'm sure you didn't want to remake the drinks."

"I know it's the south, but can you *not* act like some good old boy who cared what my boyfriend thinks? How about what *I* think?" I asked.

"Sorry, I assumed you wouldn't want frozen drinks down the front of your shirt. Katie runs a decent place — never saw her run a wet T-shirt contest or anything." He winked. "You'd win, of course."

I slapped him across the face.

The patrons gasped and I froze.

"Sorry, but that was inappropriate talk for a man so recently engaged to another woman and who calls himself sheriff," I shot back.

I marched back to the bar and avoided Katie's gaze.

"Did you just slap your ex-boyfriend?" Pete asked.

"He was never officially a boyfriend," I corrected.

Katie sauntered up next to me. "You just slapped a customer."

Luke walked over and shot me a look worse than Katie's. "We should go, Pete."

"It's not what it looked like," I defended myself.

"You slapped the sheriff," Katie added.

"But I didn't slap the deputies." I parodied that old song about shooting the sheriff, hoping for a laugh. "You're going to comp his tab anyway. I'll pay for it."

Katie leaned on the bar. "Are you okay?"

"Maybe we should drive her home?" Pete offered.

"I have my own car," I replied. "But thanks."

"We're going. Good night." Luke grabbed his brother by the arm and they left.

"Dibs on the little brother," Lurlene said.

"Why don't you go after Gus and save me the drama?" I asked.

Lurlene chuckled. "I wouldn't try to take a bone from a dog he's so attached to. That's how you get bit."

"I'm the bone...or the dog? Nice," I shot back.

"You know what I mean," she replied.

I turned to Lurlene and counted to five before I opened my mouth. "You're smarter than I gave you credit for. Gus is a mess. Maybe he's hung up on his former fiancée or maybe it's someone new, but it's not me. What guy doesn't like to play the hero?"

Lurlene lifted a dismissive shoulder. "I called dibs on the pastor's brother. Be careful or we'll be sisters-in-law."

I shared a look with Katie. "That would be something to write home about."

Katie snort-laughed. "You need to be nice to Gus. If you want to go, it's fine. Patch things up with Luke."

"No. I don't know why he's being so weird about me helping a friend, but I'm not going to act like a nun or something. I'd help my friends do anything. I mean, not rob a bank, but anything legal."

Martha laughed. "Nuns can drink. The priest from that church one town over is in at that table by the jukebox. I think the pastor is just overcompensating for something in his past by trying to make sure you look angelically perfect."

I shook my head. "I'll never be that good."

"Gus wouldn't want you to be." Lurlene winked.

"I think it's time you switched to coffee." I grabbed her a mug.

"Mean." She pouted, not really drunk yet but looking tipsy.

"You want to be able to drive home or should I call your momma? I'm sure she'll see all this and jerk you back to Jesus by your extensions." I grabbed the coffee pot.

"Drive home. I want to enjoy the music here, like you." She pointed to the coffee.

I liked the music. Gus was a good guitarist. This wasn't a trashy bar with drugs or hookers hanging out. This was a place I could bring Gran to watch the band play if she wanted. Whatever problem Luke had, we had to sort it out, because not helping my friends or family? That was wrong. Far more wrong than serving a bit of alcohol.

Lurlene said something.

"What?" I asked as I put the pot back.

"Can I get an ice water too?" she asked.

"Sure." I set out a glass of ice and grabbed the water gun. I filled the glass and poured myself one as well. "Lime or lemon?"

Lurlene waved it off.

I added a squeeze of lime to my water then added a straw.

Gus walked up to the bar. "Just checking if you're okay. My face has recovered, even if my ego is still a bit bruised."

I smiled and took a sip of water. "I'm fine, thanks. Your face got what it asked for."

"So, Sheriff, who was this fiancée?" Lurlene asked.

Gus ignored the question. "Can I get a water?"

"Sure." I grabbed him a glass and added a straw.

"You want to come up and join us?" Gus asked.

I grabbed the soda gun and fumbled it, spraying him with a seltzer water. Much as I loved music, performing left me with jitters in some venues.

"Sorry. I— No. No, thanks." I tossed a towel to him and filled the glass with water.

"The keyboard is all set up." Katie pointed.

I shook my head. "He means sing."

"The guys in the band say they've heard you singing to yourself and you're good. You're the one who let them camp on your property then works in the kitchen with the windows open. Don't get mad," he teased.

"I'm not going up there," I insisted.

Gus grabbed his water. "Our loss."

"You're going up there with a wet shirt? We're not that kind of place," Katie teased.

"I didn't bring a change of clothes. Did Miss Belle do that to get me shirtless?" he teased.

"Please, I'm surprised you're wearing shoes. You're so country you think *Deliverance* is a rom com." I wiped up the bar and ignored the teasing.

Katie grabbed for something under the bar. "This should fit you." She tossed him the same T-shirt that the employees wore.

"Thank you kindly, ma'am." He took off his cowboy hat, yanked off his wet shirt and slowly tugged on the new one.

The flashes of cameras and cat calls from women changed the feel of the room in a way I didn't personally care for.

"You're the sheriff. You know that, right—you set an example?" I taunted him.

Katie nudged me. "Be nice."

He tossed his wet shirt at my head.

I snatched it out of the air before it hit my face, but I had to admit to myself that his shirt smelled good!

Chapter Two

I hopped out of bed bright and early the next morning and got ready before the sun rose. Freshly showered and made up, I put on an old shirt and shorts for baking. All night I'd tossed and turned thinking of the Gus and Luke drama. Shirtless Gus was a nice view, but I didn't need those types of dreams.

We had a ton of fruit from local lemon trees, so I went with the obvious and made lemon cupcakes and lemon bars for after service and the shop. I checked our fruit inventory and found a lot of cranberries. As the cupcakes cooled, I whipped up lemon and cranberry muffins and put them in the hot oven. I'd add those big sugar grains once they were out of the oven to give them that fancy look and add sweetness.

The barking of my gran's new puppy signaled that they were up and moving.

"Morning," I greeted. The coffee machine fired up for a fresh pot—Gran had it programmed and had clearly synced it with her routine. Meanwhile, I started on the frosting for the cupcakes.

"Morning, dear. What are you doing?" She padded into the kitchen wearing her Tennessee Volunteer slippers and a worn old robe.

"I couldn't sleep. I wanted to get a jump on these. Hope you weren't going to use the lemons and cranberries for anything else?" I asked.

"No, it smells wonderful. We should get more cooling racks at home if you're going to go on baking binges," she said.

I folded up some boxes then tested the cupcakes and bars. They were cool enough. I gave the cupcakes a quick layer of vanilla icing and a thin layer on the bars. Then I swapped out to the lemon gel icing bag and decorated the cupcakes before giving the lemon bars a dash each.

"Sundays are busy and I'd rather have more than not enough. What else do you have too much of?" I asked.

"Mrs. Fryer dropped off a bunch of cherries, but they have to be pitted. Maybe something apple?" Gran suggested.

"That's peeling and coring—not today." I looked in the laundry room that was kept shaded and cool and blocked off from the dog. The apples looked good. We could do those tomorrow when we had a full day at work. I saw a few bunches of very yellow bananas and grabbed them.

"Banana bread?" I teased.

"I'll eat it all before we get to church." She smacked her lips and poured a cup of coffee for each of us. "How was last night?"

"Fine. Busy. Katie's place is very nice and the band is popular."

"Good. You're such a good helper. You play piano at the church and help afterward. Don't overdo it.

Sometimes you have to make choices. Luke is a good man. Handsome and nice." Gran snuck a lemon bar.

"He dropped in last night at the bar with his younger brother, Pete. Luke really doesn't seem to like it when I help out the at the bar. He always comes in to check on me," I said.

"That's nice. Sometimes drunk men are hard to handle. I know Katie has her brothers bouncing, but it's sweet for a boyfriend to worry." Gran smiled.

I frowned and added some creamer to my coffee. "No, Gran. It's not like he's visiting with people and just there if something happens. It's like he's watching me and my behavior. Like I'm there partying or getting drunk," I explained.

Gran pursed her lips. "He said to me he understood your background and that he liked how helpful you were."

"He does. I don't think it's my parents he's holding against me…he thinks I'm too wild or something. I'm not going to *not* help my friends or visit with people because it's a bar." I gave the batter a final thorough mixing before pouring it into loaf pans.

"Maybe he's thinking too far ahead too fast?" she asked.

"Meaning?" I prompted.

"Well, he can't date and *date* in his own congregation. If he's thinking marriage, then it he might be wondering if you'll cut your schedule to focus on all of the responsibilities of a pastor's wife. It's a thankless job and you don't get paid, so it's not for everyone," Gran admitted.

The oven dinged and I took out the muffins and put in the banana bread.

"Am I wrong?" she asked.

"No, I wasn't thinking that far into it. We weren't that serious."

"But he has to be or people will think he's taking advantage of a lot of young women. Just think of it like that and let him know how you feel about it. Balancing your work with me at the shop, helping with all the church events and outreaches and helping your friends — something will have to give. I can do the shop alone, but you seem to love it," Gran said.

"No, the shop is our business. I'm not giving that up. I'm not giving up my friends or helping when they need a hand. They've been there for me when I needed help. If he just wants a wife to take on a lot of work he should be doing or volunteers are doing, then he's after a wife for the wrong reasons," I said.

"Men's lives generally are made easier by marriage. Cooking, cleaning and all that social stuff — it's just what women do." Gran sighed.

I shook my head. "Running a family is one thing. An unpaid church job and all the wife work? No thanks."

"Talk to him before you jump to any conclusions or reactions."

I nodded. "I know you're right. With how my mom was, I'm probably better off being a single career woman. We'll franchise this thing and have our own show on the cooking channel."

Gran tested a muffin. "Sure, dear. Whatever you want."

Assessing my leftovers, I made a banana and cranberry loaf and tossed it into the oven then took the banana bread out to cool. I started packing up the cool treats for transport. Finally, I set some of the lemon stuff aside for the shop afterward.

"You're not happy," Gran said.

"I'm just thinking right now," I replied.

She finished her cup of coffee then put it in the sink. "Well, it's important to find out what makes people tick. If he's more interested in appearances than substance, you need to be rid of him. If he's in a real rush, also get rid of him."

I'd never expected Gran to say 'dump the pastor', but that was exactly what she'd advised. She didn't want to see me make a mistake and end up divorced quickly. I wasn't going to rush into anything.

* * * *

After the Sunday morning church service, I set out the treats and helped open the food pantry. Harry, one of Katie's brothers, drove up in a big refrigerated truck.

"Never look a gift horse in the mouth, but what's going on?" I asked.

Martha grinned. "The grocery store owner decided to donate anything getting close to expiration. They know the rules and that you don't have storage, so they sent it over today and people can decide what they want, what they'll be able to use safely before it's officially expired. Harry offered to drive it over and bring back what doesn't go and it'll end up in the dumpster."

"That's very nice. A little notice would've helped us to organize this. I hope we have enough men to help unload. No one will want to ruin their Sunday clothes," I teased.

Martha had dressed up a little extra. "Harry's brothers and the deputies are here. Gus made a show of his muscles at the bar—he'll help." Martha smiled.

I rolled my eyes at her. "It was an accident. I shouldn't be allowed to tend bar unless it's coffee. No one would let me waitress ever."

"Or ice cream," one of Martha's daughters piped up.

"Ice cream bar? I like the sound of that," I replied.

Luke walked up. "This is a blessing."

"Very kind. The Heavenly Hazelnut is the flavor of the day, if you want to swing by the shop after," I suggested.

"My favorite. Thanks, but my brother wants to see some of the town. We'll see if we have time to stop in. I would like to have dinner tonight, if you're free," he offered.

"Sure. Where?" I asked.

"I'll text you. I'm not sure. I'll get reservations somewhere nice," he said.

"With your brother?" I asked.

"No, he made some friends already. He'll probably be the bar or over in Nashville. Just us." Luke smiled.

He was handsome and nice. The guy was solid and comfortable talking to lots of people, but that didn't mean he was right for me.

"Okay, let me know." I went back to helping inventory the items as they came off the truck.

Martha was blushing and flirting with Harry, and the men went to work bringing the products down. It'd be helpful for the families.

One of the choir ladies walked up. "All this eggs and cream—I might do my own baking," she joked.

"Any little bit helps, right, Megan?" I asked. "If wishes were horses, I guess the poor are riding today."

She was a member of the choir, so I knew her well enough that she was on the food pantry list. A nice single woman who needed a better job and was looking in Nashville. I felt bad for her.

"Absolutely. Have you seen Shelley?" she asked.

"No, not this week at all." I shrugged. She had two kids, so it was hard to miss her if they'd attended service. "Maybe one of the kids is sick?"

Megan muttered something that sounded like vague agreement then moved on to get some of the donated dairy stuff.

Gran shuffled up to me. "I think we need to go back to the shop. Get the stuff going."

"Okay, let's go."

"You're not going to say goodbye to the pastor?" she asked.

"He's busy. We have dinner plans. I'll deal with things then," I reassured her.

Gran checked her phone but said nothing.

* * * *

The day had flown by, with lemon goodies being more popular than I'd imagined. Primped and put together for a nice place, I had no idea where I was going, so I'd had to put it in my phone GPS. I parked my well-worn white pickup outside of a nice Italian-style restaurant then touched up my lipstick.

I saw his car and took a deep breath. We'd only been dating a few weeks, so I wasn't expecting anything, but I did need to figure him out a bit more to see if I was wasting my time. Maybe he had our relationship on the fast track and I was still warming up.

I walked in and he spotted me. He stood up at the back booth so I could find him. Luke had very gentlemanly manners most of the time — when we were alone. The hostess walked me back and set out a menu.

Luke kissed me on the cheek.

"Did you have a good afternoon?" I asked.

He nodded. "My brother is a good guy and his profession is very caring, but sometimes he hangs out with men with bad habits."

"A couple drinks isn't that bad when you have the night off," I replied.

"I know. He just doesn't plan. He drops in without even calling." Luke's jaw tensed.

"That is a bit rude. But when you jump at an alarm and have to be ready for any emergency, I guess you're good to at the drop of a hat. Maybe he got the time and it's nice he wanted to see you." I flipped through the menu and picked something new.

"Good day at the shop?" Luke asked.

"Very. People love that hazelnut smoothie and all the lemon items were popular," I said.

He frowned.

"That's bad?" I asked.

"No, I just hate that you don't have a day off. You're in that shop seven days a week. Sunday is for rest and family," he scolded.

The waitress moved in and took our order, so I had a few breaths to collect my thoughts. I took a sip of water.

"You're saying we should close the shop on Sunday?" I asked.

"Well, you could hire people to work those days, if you must," he replied.

"You obviously work on Sunday," I countered.

"I have to, and that way we could spend the day together. You're good with people and like to help." He shrugged.

"If we become profitable enough to have more employees, rotating the schedules so everyone gets two days off a week is definitely a goal. But Gran generally chats with people, especially on Sundays, so I don't think it's unfair to her. I love the shop so it doesn't feel like work," I explained.

"We need to talk about a few things if this is going to be serious," he said as he fidgeted with his silverware.

"I agree. You coming to the bar and acting like I'm dancing on the tables or stripping instead of helping my friend with her business is *not* okay."

He sat back and looked a little stunned. "My brother wanted to meet you. I'm not a fan of bars, but I admire your work ethic and helping a friend."

"It still felt like you were there checking up on me," I said.

He looked around. "Other men in the club might be bothering you."

I chuckled. "I can handle myself. Katie's brothers are like my brothers. They'd protect me no matter what. It's a safe small town."

He drummed his fingers on the bar. "I think it looks better if your boyfriend is with you."

"You think that will fix my reputation? My parents' story? You can't change who I am or whitewash over it." Maybe he thought I was dating him to change how people looked at me?

"I do care about you and like you, Belle. I wanted to help and see if we were compatible," he admitted.

Help? I took a long drink of water. "No, I don't think we are compatible. If you're going to disapprove of me helping my friend or working on a Sunday at my own business, no. I'm not trying to become a saint. I want people to judge me for me, not my parents. And not by you. I'm clearly not cut out to be a pastor's girlfriend or wife."

"I wanted to help, but you're a rebel. It's in your blood," he teased.

29

"Rebel? Life is a game played with marked cards," I shot back. "Help is a bad thing?"

"You think you have all the answers. That everyone needs you. Your gran needs you, of course, but Katie and everyone else around managed just fine before you returned to town. It's not an invitation for you to change up everything. You meddled with a murder investigation because you thought you knew how to do it better," he said.

"No, I had information and access the new sheriff didn't," I defended myself.

"And it only grows. You move Martha around so she's working in three places now? She's a mother," Luke scolded.

"And her ex isn't exactly generous in supporting his kids. She needs the money and he should spend more time with his kids. She only works at my shop or the bar when she has childcare and it works for her. If you're that old-fashioned, we'd never work as a couple," I countered.

"What? Because I want children to have their mother?" he asked.

"They have their mother. You want all the women to stay home with the kids and only dads work? That's not possible, not in this world. I wouldn't want that to be the expectation or rule either. Wow, this was a major mistake." I slid from the booth and stood.

"It's what women really want. A man to support and take care of them and their kids. They can work on charity and help others. Women wanting to take over and boss around men is why the world is going to hell," he said.

"You're insane. What about abusive men or cheaters? Women should just tolerate it?" I stood toe-to-toe with him — sometimes I couldn't back down.

"Men can change and be forgiven. Women like that should rely on their families for help," he explained.

"You're nothing like I thought you were. What about me? My father ran off, my grandfather died. There are no brothers or uncles to count on. Should Gran and I go begging?" I asked.

"That's why I was trying to help you. There is potential in you. Your grandmother did nothing wrong. Life can be unfair, but you're a rebel deep down. I did my best to help but you're not willing to change." He shook his head.

"Help? Help by dating? By making my family respectable. You took pity on me in your warped perception of this?" I asked.

Luke sighed. "I tried. You could've had a good life as a pastor's wife. Your gran would have her shop and be respected in the town. The pity would go away with one wedding. You think you don't need me, but you can't do it by yourself."

Help. Pity. Respect. My hands trembled as I realized how badly I'd misjudged the situation. I grabbed my glass of water and splashed it in his face.

"We're done. I'd rather become a groupie for that band and follow them around the south than date you for another second."

I stalked out of the restaurant, hungry and pissed off.

"Men! Like licking honey off a thorn." I slammed the door to my pickup and peeled out of the parking lot.

Chapter Three

I'd hidden out in the back of the shop for most of Monday. A public break-up scene wasn't exactly the image I was going for. Who dumps a pastor like that? Word had spread despite everyone saying Luke hadn't been seen in public all day. His car was parked in front of his home.

Tuesday morning, I refused to hide. The morning rush was crazy. Most people just asked how I was doing.

"Fine. Mr. Right is hard to find," became my standard answer.

"If you need to take a break, we're good." Martha had come in before her grocery store shift to help out.

"I'm fine, thanks. I can't thank you enough for helping out yesterday. Luke might be taking the high road, too, but I can't avoid people forever," I said.

Martha nodded. "True. The girls had a blast baking with you in the back. Free babysitting and we took home the imperfect loaves."

"You girls are all single again. You should get on an app," Gran suggested.

"Why is Katie single? She's gorgeous, always around men and outgoing," Martha asked.

Gran sighed. "Her poor mother was very unlucky in love. She tried hard, made the men marry her—she wasn't a bad girl. But things never worked out. Katie saw that. I think she's afraid of making the same mistakes. If you don't have a good example of a healthy relationship, how do you know when it's worth working at or not and it's time to cut and run at the first sign of trouble?"

"She does have a good business. Marry the wrong man and get divorced, he might want a piece of it," Martha speculated.

"Exactly. Her success makes her a target for men who want to sit around and do nothing. I have no objection to a stay-at-home dad situation, but some men want a mommy." Gran sighed.

I was distracted and the coffee cup overflowed a bit. "Darn." I pulled my hand away.

"Oh, Belle, I didn't mean that had anything to do with you and the pastor. He's a caveman. Certainly not the right man for you. It was the right call...just a bit public," Gran advised.

"I know. I was lucky to get to see you and Grandpa be so happy. Katie will find the right guy. She might test him like the ten plagues, but the right man will prove himself. Good men are hard to find, harder these days."

Gran shook her head. Her group of four guys who acted like they helped around the shop were at their usual table. Gran sat with them when things were quiet.

"I can't believe he let you go," called out Milan, one of Gran's admirers.

"We weren't a good fit," I argued.

Martha re-poured the coffee I'd spilled and wiped up the counter. "It's weird, though. Normally Pastor Luke does his shopping every Monday morning, like clockwork. Then he has lunch with a couple of the volunteers and staff. I worked the register from opening until two and he never came into the grocery store."

"He could've skipped it to avoid the talk," Milan suggested.

"He's ashamed of himself. He should be." Gran wagged her finger.

I shook my head. "That's not how people are telling it. But I did lose my temper. I yelled and threw my water in his face."

"And he deserved it." Martha nodded.

"Thanks for the support. It's over and I'm free to focus on my shop and my friends." I felt lighter. It was the right choice, even if I could've been more dignified about it. "He's a lot more conservative in a lot of ways that I thought a younger man wouldn't be, even a pastor."

"Oh, there are threads of real deep conservatives all over the south. Gotta watch your modern views there, young lady," Joe said.

"I lived in Atlanta for a while, but it's not like I'm walking around naked and telling people not to go church." I frowned.

Gran scoffed. "I'd smack you upside the head and cover you with one of my old house dresses."

"You never know someone until you spend a lot of time with them. Even if you marry them, sometimes they aren't honest until it's too late." Martha restocked the cups and cleaned one of the machines while the shop was slow.

"Your ex is an idiot. You're so nice and hardworking," I teased.

She smiled. "But when you're the one doing all the work without help—it's awful. Might as well just be a single parent."

Gran reorganized the pastries we had left. "If you ever feel like we're working you too much, you just say no. Some women never learn to use that word and mean it. Moms need to take care of themselves too."

"I didn't mean you. I love working here and the bar. It's a nice variety and I can use the extra cash tips. My mom is actually proud of me and helping by watching the girls more." Martha smiled and gave Gran a hug.

"Independence isn't a four-letter word!" I declared. "Marry a handsome man and you marry trouble."

Gus and Lou, one of the deputies, came in the shop.

"What's your poison?" I asked.

When they took off their hats, I knew something weird was up. Touching the brim or tipping their hats might be good old southern manners, but taking them off…

"What's wrong?" Martha asked.

"You had dinner with Pastor Luke Sunday night?" Gus asked.

I blushed. "Not exactly. We didn't make it to dinner. We broke up."

"But you saw him and he was fine when you left?" Gus asked.

"Yes, I drove off and he was sitting at the table. I haven't talked to him since, but I don't want to. Doubt he'd want to speak to me. That's over," I said.

The edges of Gus' mouth quivered a bit but he didn't actually crack a smile.

"I've been looking for his brother, but he's staying at the motel on the edge of town and wasn't answering. We need to start an investigation. I'm sorry to inform you that Luke is dead."

Martha dropped a coffee mug. "Sorry."

"Dead?" Part of me wanted to laugh. Was this a joke? Before it was the sheriff, now Luke? We don't have that many deaths in a small town like Sweet Grove. *Was it a car crash?* Luke was young and healthy.

Martha cleaned up the pieces. "What happened?"

"Please heavens, let him be okay," Gran prayed.

"Gran, the sheriff said that Luke is dead, not missing," I reminded her.

"The church secretary called us when she'd been trying to contact the pastor for most of Monday when he didn't come into the office or call. His car is clearly in his driveway but he's not answering the home phone or his cell." Gus sighed.

"I haven't tried to call, but he hasn't called me." I pulled my phone out of my pocket.

Gus waved away my phone. "I believe you. The home is technically the property of the church, so we got the okay and entered. Any ideas what we found?"

I grabbed my water bottle and took a drink. "Luke, dead."

"How?" Milan asked.

"First we found something else. Which is why we're pretty sure you're not involved. But it's a bit confusing," Lou said.

"I don't understand. What else did you find?" I asked.

"I'm confused too," Gran agreed.

Lou showed me a picture on his phone. I moved back.

"A snake? A rattler got in his house?"

Gus shook his head.

"People can be allergic, if he was and got bitten—he very well could've died before he could even call for help," Martha said.

"That's not a rattler," Gus argued.

I frowned and looked closer. "It's not a cottonmouth or coral." Those were the snakes we'd grown up learning about as kids. They were the dangerous ones.

"We got Animal Control on the scene now. They believe it's a Burmese Python. From the looks of Luke, he was crushed around the torso."

"Wait, don't those snakes eat what they kill?" Milan asked.

Lou nodded. "According to the research, they do. There were bite marks on the body."

I shuddered and Martha gasped. Gran sat down at the table with her guys.

"I saw something about that on one of the nature channels. The snake's jaw can't open wide enough to swallow the human shoulders." Martha shuddered.

"Please stop." I took another drink of water. "How big is that snake?"

"About four feet and a good two inches around. Not near fully grown but strong enough to kill a man. Some people keep them as pets," Gus said.

"No one I know." I shook my head. "I'm sorry, I don't know anyone who wanted Luke dead."

"You get the timing is unfortunate," he said.

"I couldn't handle a four-foot snake of any kind. Luke and I didn't work out, but I didn't want him dead," I answered.

"A bad break-up could be viewed as a motive. We can't rule you out because you say it was amicable. Any ideas who would? Luke having any problems with money or people?" Gus asked.

I folded my arms and took a deep breath. "He brought his brother to the bar, but you know that. He's in town for a bit. They didn't seem super close, but coming to town and meeting everyone just to kill your brother doesn't really make sense."

"No, it doesn't. He wasn't having trouble with anyone in the church?" Gus asked.

I frowned. "He didn't tell me about counseling sessions or stuff like that. I know deep down he's more conservative than he tries to appear most of the time. He didn't like me working in a bar, even if my friend owns it. I'm not sure what else I don't know about him, but I found out enough to know we weren't a good match."

"My friend Lolly Mae moved to Florida. They have a lot of those types of snakes down there in those swamp areas. Maybe they're just on the move? Or someone had it for a pet and it got loose? It could all be an accident," Gran suggested.

"We've put the word out, but no one's reported a lost pet snake," Lou said.

"The pastor's house was newer and well-maintained. If a snake got in there, odds are it'd be a harmless type or an eastern diamondback. But he's not on the outskirts with acres and acres of land. The house is near the church. When's the last time you've seen a snake in town?" Gus asked.

"Never, now. In my back yard, a few. I whack 'em with the shovel," Gran admitted.

"Hopefully it's only one snake and nothing else," Martha added.

Gus' phone rang and he stepped outside to take the call.

"Sorry, Lou, can I get you a coffee or water?" I offered.

"Not right now, thanks," Lou answered.

"Belle, you should sit down," Martha said.

I shook my head but took another drink of water. "We only dated for a few weeks. It was very casual, nothing serious. What's the old saying? You never know the length of a snake until it's dead. Why did that pop in my head?"

Gus walked in and looked relieved. "They have the snake and it's still alive for now. There were no other animals in the home. We can go over there and photograph, get any evidence, but the coroner is on the way as well. Let's go, Lou."

"You guys want to take some coffee and rolls for all the people?" I offered.

He grinned at me. "Probably should. Thanks."

Lou and Gran went over to get the pastries while Martha and I set up ten coffees to go with sugar and creamer they could add later. Not our fanciest, but practical.

"I know you didn't do it, but I have to ask," Gus said.

"I went straight home. Gran was sitting up watching TV," I replied.

He reached for his wallet.

"No charge for cops," I reminded him.

"Thanks. Anyone else see you come home? Gran is not impartial," Gus said.

"She's not a liar," Martha butted in.

I patted her arm. "It's okay. Can you get Lou a bigger bag?"

Martha slipped in the back.

"The band may have been home. Sunday nights are line dance lessons at the bar. Pretty slow. They might've been out drinking, but I think there were lights on in the RV. They may have seen me pull up," I suggested.

As if to save my nerves, the band members all rolled into the shop.

"What brings you boys here?" Gran asked.

Dillon hugged her. "We're going to an audition in Nashville this afternoon and we'll be back for our set at the Buckle. But we wanted the best food in town and a kiss for luck."

Gran blushed and kissed each of the band guys on the cheek.

Martha helped Lou bag up some muffins then got on the band's order.

"Hey, guys," I said.

Gus patted my hand. "I'll ask."

I felt like no one trusted me. Obviously, my taste in men was wildly suspect, but I wasn't a killer.

Dillon and the band talked to Gus.

Gus walked over to me. "They confirmed an estimated time when you got home. Based on the drive from the restaurant and traffic levels, your whereabouts are confirmed for that night. We'll round up some witnesses from the restaurant to be sure when you left."

"That'll be easy. Half the staff and plenty of diners saw. I bet they have cameras that cover the parking lots too. I did throw water in his face, but he was being a sexist jerk on top of pitying me." I bit my lower lip. Everything coming out of my mouth was potentially viewable as motive.

"We'll check it all out. If I were you, I'd stay out of this for now. I'll come back to interview you more later."

"Okay, I understand." I nodded.

"Sorry for your loss," he said.

"Okay. I feel bad for his brother." I fought to keep my composure like a proper southern lady with all the conflicting feelings going on inside me. Finally, I understood the desire to faint on cue.

"You needed an alibi. Belle, I knew you were a bad girl," Dillon teased.

"Yes, bad girls break up with the pastor. But I don't own a snake or know anyone who does. So it wasn't me. I got out of that relationship before I had anything to really be pissed at him about," I explained.

"We told him the truth. We saw you go in the back door. The driveway angles so headlights hit the RV. We keep meaning to move it but then we forget. You were hotter than a rattler in a room full of rocking chairs. Never heard a woman slam a car door so hard." Dillon winked.

I shook my head. "I'm a career girl now. Nine to five or twenty-four-seven."

The guys kicked off an acapella version of Dolly Parton's song that made everyone laugh and clap. This was very distasteful considering the news of Luke's death, but sometimes people needed to smile and right now I needed it.

Once they were gone, Gran walked over and patted my shoulder. "You know you're still a suspect in the town? Gus might believe you and try to clear you, but this won't look good. People aren't as nice as Gus."

I smiled weakly. "This one has got to be easier to solve. Who has access to that sort of a snake?"

"I asked one of the band guys that. Those are very easy to get. Tons of those snakes got let loose and are breeding in in the wetlands of Florida. Pet shops will sell them as babies, ship them all over — illegally — and there you go. I'm sure there's some illegal snake dealer in Nashville. Anyone willing could've gotten their hands on one. That person had to be crazy," Gran said.

"I need to make sure I turned off the oven. I'll be right back." I slipped into the kitchen.

In the back, alone, I took a deep breath and blotted my eyes. I hadn't been going to marry him and he hadn't been the right guy for me. But Luke hadn't deserved to die. Taking a deep breath, I held my head up. I was innocent—I wasn't really a suspect this time, but I knew some wouldn't simply accept my word. I'd be easy to blame and I had been very publicly seen with him the last time he'd been seen alive.

Bottom line, I'd have to help find the killer to prove I was in the clear. Working with Gus could be painful—I'd never exactly figured out my feelings for him when his ex-fiancée had shown up and flung a ring around. But if I had to prove my innocence, at least Gus believed in it too.

I went out front and word was already spreading. A couple who had come in were shaking their heads. They shot me a look.

"I can't believe anyone would hurt the pastor," she said.

"Clearly someone wanted him dead. Plenty of harmless but scary-looking snakes to slip in someone's place if you just want to spook them," Milan replied.

"He wasn't the man I thought he was when he asked me out. Even pastors have secrets," I agreed.

Chapter Four

The news spread all over town. I never left the shop, working and trying to digest the information. People gave me odd looks as they came and went, but no one was rude. I also worked the kitchen a lot so I had some breathing room.

I made another batch of Gran's bread and whipped up a triple batch of corn bread. Looking for a project, I inventoried what we had and checked expiration dates. The profits were still slim and I wasn't going to waste anything.

Gran came back and gently closed the fridge.

"I'm sorry. It's still a shock," she said.

"I wasn't in love with him or anything. Honestly, I was more into Gus before. I just can't believe Luke is gone. Like that. The irony and the creep factor."

"Irony?" Gran asked.

"A pastor killed by a snake. That's a touch of the old Garden of Eden, right?" I asked.

Gran hugged me. "I hadn't thought about it. That's why you're so good at figuring out who did it when I watch *Father Brown* or my other mystery shows. You and Gus will solve it in no time."

"I don't want to encourage him. I have bad taste in men, clearly. I meant what I said. Career. This shop is our legacy and it will succeed. Our house might be on the modest side of town, but we have land and a business. I don't need to have a husband." I took a deep breath.

"No, you don't. But you wouldn't go out with a pastor if you didn't want a good man in your life. I'm proud of you for not acting like Lurlene…all desperate for a wedding. Just don't shut yourself off. I'm sure there's a story with Gus and his ex-fiancée. There's always more than one side. When you're ready, you'll hear it. Maybe he's not the one either, but snap judgments do no one credit," Gran warned.

"He had plenty of time to tell me about her when he was flirting with me," I reasoned.

"Agreed, but men aren't perfect. Plus, we all want to put our best foot forward when flirting in the beginning. You'll see each other as human with flaws and bad choices soon enough. Don't hide in here all afternoon. That corn bread smells like it's done, by the way," she said.

"I'll check on it and be right out." I smiled.

Before I got my oven mitts on, the oven dinged. Gran's nose was priceless.

I walked out with fresh corn bread to Martha chatting with Megan from the church.

"Hi," I greeted.

"Hi," Megan replied.

"Do you need me for the afternoon? Sally is still MIA and they need someone to fill in at the grocery store," Martha said.

"No, we're pretty slow. Word is getting around." I frowned.

"Word?" Megan asked. "Oh, about Sally. It's probably nothing. She left a message with the boss she was taking her kids to visit family up in Indiana while her hubby was on some extra-long haul. But she's been gone two weeks and not a peep since. She won't answer her phone. The school hasn't heard about when little Christy or Ed Junior will return. We're starting to worry but not panic just yet. We're hoping she got away somewhere safe for good."

"Got away from what?" I asked.

"You really aren't a gossip. I thought maybe you'd helped her. Her husband is abusive. She hides the bruises really well and he never touched the children that we've heard of. Still, she had me holding some money for her to run off with and we'd all add to it when we could," Megan explained.

Just when you thought you knew people. "That's so great. I would've helped if I knew. Did she ask for the money?"

"No, that's the odd part. Maybe she got a chance to move in with relatives but had to move fast or was worried her hubby might notice something strange. Controlling men like that are terrifying. They'll check gas tanks, bank accounts, and have a friend watch their wife. Not that Ed has any friends." Megan chuckled.

"None. What a jerk. Makes any guy who doesn't hit women look like a prince, which is terrible, but..." Martha sighed. "I'll take the shift."

"Thanks. I'm not feeling so good. Super queasy. I hope it's not the flu," she said.

"Can I ask who her hubby was? I don't think I've met Ed, but I'm sure I've seen them in church," I remarked.

"You saw Sally in church with her little girl and son. Big Ed never bothered. Shaved head, ink on his arms, leather vest," Martha replied.

"Oh, I've seen him in the bar." I nodded.

"That's Big Ed. Don't get in his way. He'll be gone on another trucker haul soon enough. He's not a nice drunk, either. I'm going to get a Heavenly Hazelnut smoothie and a big hunk of corn bread, please. Maybe that'll settle my stomach." Megan smiled.

Martha served up the corn bread and pulled out the blender.

"Belle," Martha said.

"Yeah?" I asked. The request for the pastor's favorite smoothie threw my emotions into weird places.

"I can't reach the smoothie stuff. Can you move, please?" Martha asked.

"Sure. Sorry. Long day." I moved to the coffee side and pulled out a stool we tucked under the register for Gran. Sitting, I made myself an iced coffee. Maybe I'd wake myself from this crazy nightmare.

Whether I'd been close to the victim or not, whether I was involved in any way with the capture of the killer or not...we'd had another murder in our tiny southern town.

Megan got her goodies. "Thanks, and thanks again for taking the shift, Martha. I think we need to plan around Sally for now."

"Absolutely, I'm happy to do it. But when you're feeling better, you take on as many as you like. Don't let others push you out. And let me know if you hear from her that she's safe." Martha waved.

Once Megan was gone, Martha turned away from the door and took off her apron. "I feel terrible."

"Why? We're quiet in the afternoons anyway. Everyone is talking about the pastor. It's fine." I waved it off.

"No, Megan doesn't know about the pastor. You could tell or she'd be talking about that. Hell, she'll be a mess," Martha said.

Gran picked up her head. "Language. Not in the shop, please."

"Sorry, Mrs. Baxter. Megan always had a crush on the pastor. I thought maybe they'd become an item, but it never happened. She'll be a wreck. I'm going to grab my purse and use the washroom before I head out." Martha ducked in the back.

She wasn't there ten seconds before we heard a scream. I darted back there. Rolling pin in hand, Gran was behind me with her motley crew of suitors.

"Martha," I called.

"Snake." She stood outside the employee rest room and pointed. Luckily she hadn't gone in and closed the door, or she'd be trapped.

"I got it." Milan pulled a pistol from his ankle.

"No, you'll hit the pipes," I warned.

"Ladies, this is men's work," Milan insisted.

He took a shot while I grabbed the rolling pin from Gran and tried to convince her to go up front.

"Belle, we have to catch it. We'll be shut down by the health department if we don't," Gran argued as she picked up an empty five-gallon bucket.

The rattler coiled tight with all the talking.

"Just hold still," Milan warned.

"The back door was open. Someone might've done it on purpose," Martha suggested.

Milan popped off another .22 caliber round and the snake reacted to the noise. Without thinking, I swung the rolling pin into its path and the snake chomped on the wood. I dropped it and looked for something else to defend us with.

But genius Gran got there first, slamming the bucket down on the snake. Within seconds, the bucket started to move.

"Belle, you sit on this thing now," Gran ordered.

I sat on the bucket before the snake managed to knock it over or make a slithery escape.

"You call Gus and I'll call Animal Control," Milan said.

"So much for your marksmanship," Martha teased.

Milan shrugged. "With my arthritis, all I can do is try."

"No, you can't try to hit things with a bullet. You need to be able to hit them or don't fire the gun," I corrected.

Gran scoffed. "Men around here act like guns are attached to them. I'll go cover the front until you're done here."

Just then we heard, "Animal Control," shouted from the front.

"Back here," we all shouted in return.

"That was quick." I breathed a sigh of relief.

"Small-town service, you can't beat it in an emergency," Gran said.

* * * *

When the snake was captured, Gus had his report, and the bucket and my rolling pin were in the trash— can't use something that was in contract with rattlesnake venom, no way—we were nearly back to normal.

Martha got ready to leave again but my brain had been working overtime while I was sitting on that dumb bucket. I held up my hand. "On Sunday, Megan was taking stuff from the food pantry and said something about trying to get more hours. It's really weird that she gave up a shift to you if she could use the money."

"It's not odd if she feels sick…you can't work with the stomach flu. She could make other people sick," Gran commented.

"If you need the money that badly, you work sick. But if she got enough from the pantry to hold her over—maybe she feels that bad?" Martha pondered. "I'll tell my mom to give her Sally's shifts as much as possible. That might put her almost at a full timer."

"Will they hold Sally's job?" Gran asked.

"No call, no show? Once she runs out of time off, she's gone. My mom is a manager, but you can't have one set of rules for everyone else and make exceptions for one. I hope she found a safe place to go and doesn't come back. They'll be better off without him," Martha said. "I have to go pick up the kids, get them home and change for the store. Bye. Thanks."

"Bye, thank you, dear," Gran called.

* * * *

I headed to the bar after dinner. Gran didn't ask and I didn't offer the fact that I wasn't working. I helped set up anyway. I'd been raised to be helpful. Besides, cutting fruit and wiping down tables wasn't a big deal.

Katie walked in late and hugged me.

"Where have you been?" I asked.

She smiled. "I had a meeting with our liquor vendor. Trying to get better prices on what we use more of. I heard about the pastor, though. Are you okay?"

"Yes, thanks. I dumped him Sunday night, so I'm in the middle. But it was a snake."

"I heard. Pythons crush. I had a boyfriend who had a boa constrictor once. Those go for the neck more. The freaky pets people can have." Katie tied an apron around her waist and headed for the bar. "Just lie low and let Gus sort it out. You didn't like it when my brother found those little garter snakes in the yard and wanted to show them off. You'd never touch a big or dangerous snake."

"No. I wouldn't, but I do have to help find the killer. I can't let people think I was in on it. I can't let another murder suspicion hurt the shop or Gran's reputation," I said.

"Belle, stop. You're not behind it. Someone had a big grudge against him to do that. I mean, why wouldn't the pastor just have left as soon as he saw it? Why didn't he call for help?" Katie asked.

"I don't know. Gus was investigating the crime scene with the coroner. Maybe it was kept in the bathroom or locked in the shower. His house only has one bathroom and I used it once when he showed me around the place. There was a bathtub and a shower, but the shower was square, small. From the floor to about shoulder height, it was ceramic tile. The door was white. Above the shoulder, the shower walls were glass all the way to the ceiling and there was a noisy fan. It was odd but functional."

"Why would you need to run the fan?" she asked.

"Don't you always run the fan in a bathroom when you pee around a guy for the first few times?" I asked.

"True. That shower could've held the snake for a bit, but it'd push on the door. Those aren't exactly hard to open," Katie pointed out.

I nodded. "Tie the handle to something with enough strength. Like the tub. It was old cast iron with clawed feet. Heavy."

Katie laughed. "You're so good at this. Don't be too good or they'll think you did it. Wait until you see what Gus has to say. Whatever they found and where."

"Please, we had a rattler in the back of the shop today. Someone is trying to set me up or scare more people. Maybe hurt more." I went behind the bar and practiced my girlie shot flavors. Then I tested one.

"A rattler. But you're okay. Belle, are you working tonight?" Katie asked.

"Nope, not on the schedule. Yes, we're all safe from the snake. Unless you need me to work, I don't mind. I'm just practicing for that class," I said.

Katie walked up and leaned on the bar as I tested a cherry cinnamon creation. "Making up your own drinks isn't part of the class."

"Maybe I'm gifted?" I asked and tested an Irish cream with espresso liquor shot. "Nice. Makes the snake memories go away."

"You need to stop. You had nothing to do with it. You texted me for an hour Sunday night after you dumped him about how he wasn't what he pretended to be. We talked this out. He wasn't good for you. That's not a reason to feel guilty. You didn't hurt him. He definitely didn't treat you the way you deserved. Don't get twisted up in feelings and *what if*s plus liquor," she warned.

"I'm just trying to numb a little of the feelings. If I hadn't broken up with him that night, maybe he'd be alive? Maybe something would've changed and they couldn't get the snake in his house," I wondered aloud.

"I understand, but you're a lightweight," Katie warned. "Switch to wine or a margarita, easy on the rum."

"Okay," I said.

"And hydrate. I have to go in the back and check on something. You're okay?" she asked.

"Okay. Should I open?"

"Yeah, sure. Harry will be here soon to work the door," Katie replied. "I'll be right back."

"Got it." I did the last two tester shots once the kitchen door swung closed. The flush feeling was nice. Pain and anxiety gone.

I put the glasses in the dirty bin and walked over to the main door. Turning the locks with one hand, I flipped the outside lights on with the other. I used my hip to open the door and saw Harry walking up.

"Hey, you're the door guy." I gave him a hug.

"You're not feeling the pain. You okay?" he asked.

"I am. I'm not working, just helping, sort of." I smiled.

"Okay. Go inside and get some potato wedges and a Diet Coke while I watch the door?" he suggested.

"Diet Coke." I shot him a look.

He laughed. "Milkshake, I don't care. Eat something, and no more alcohol."

"Why not? That's what a bar is for," Pete teased as he walked in.

I went back to the bar and poured myself a Diet Coke. "What can I get you? I'm so sorry about your brother."

Pete nodded. "Thanks. I don't know who would do that or want to. Do you? I'm sorry, no. I can't put you in that position. Gus is investigating. But a little lady like you, I can't imagine you handling a snake. Though there are women who do that sort of thing and handle snakes bigger than they are."

"I'm not one of them. I'm not good with snakes or reptiles in general. Luke and I broke up, so I'm sure a lot of people are going to be giving me the side-eye."

"I get it. He called me that night. He was pissed and confused. My brother never got the *judge not* part of religion. He figured there's right and wrong. He'd forgive and help anyone to repent, but he had to hammer home the right versus wrong. Guilt was necessary. But even a pastor isn't perfect." Pete shook his head.

"What can I get you?" I offered.

"Are you working?"

"I can pour," I offered.

"Four shots of whiskey, thanks."

I set up the glasses and picked up the house bottle. "Good?" I asked.

"Fine. My brother never drank unless someone else was paying," Pete quipped.

I laughed. "He was on the frugal side. I should've stuck it out through dinner and dumped him after the expensive restaurant."

"No, you're too good to do that." Pete lifted his first shot. "To my late brother."

I lifted my Diet Coke.

"No, do a shot," he encouraged.

"No, I already did a few."

Pete tapped the bar. "One toast to my brother."

I lifted the shot glass.

"He wasn't perfect, but he was family."

We clinked the glasses together, then I downed mine fast. The grimace on my face must've given away my girlie drink preferences.

"Sorry, not your thing." He laughed.

"No, so the other two are yours. I'm done." I popped a few cherries into my mouth and chewed, then squeezed a lime wedge into my Diet Coke and took a sip.

The band set up and came over for waters.

"You could sing something," Pete suggested.

"No," I scoffed and laughed. "Merit might be superior to birth, but virtue is not hereditary."

"Oh, Belle's had a couple drinks," Dillon teased.

"Toasting the pastor," I explained.

"You sure you don't want to sing?" he asked.

I shook my head. "How did your audition go?"

"Even with a few drinks, she remembers everything." Dillon sighed.

"I do," I admitted.

"The audition was okay. We have to wait and see. You could cheer us up by singing," Dillon teased.

I pouted and looked at the stage. "No way. Too much going on."

"What would you sing if you did?" Pete asked.

I shook my head.

"No pressure. I'm just asking what you'd sing?" Pete asked.

I smiled slightly. "*Any Man of Mine*."

"Good song. Crossover and sassy." Dillon winked.

"And not appropriate now. It's what I sang in college when friends dragged me to do karaoke. Go set up." I waved them off.

Half an hour later, I'd added a little rum to the Diet Coke and was sitting at the bar, not behind it. When Lurlene came in, I looked for an escape route.

Heading for the door, I texted for a ride service or something.

"Belle Baxter, want to do one before you leave?" Dillon asked from the stage.

I tried to keep going but someone blocked me.

I walked over to the stage. "No, I'm good."

"Come on." They started playing the song.

Small-town me said *no!* College and tipsy me screamed in my head *That's our song!*

I made it up on stage without falling or puking, so I took the mic. It was a bad idea, I knew it. It was the wrong song for the situation. I needed to be upbeat, but it was awful…people would talk.

I wrapped up the song and Dillon teased another. Just then I saw Gus headed for the stage. I dodged musicians and headed for the front door.

While I was on my phone looking for a ride, Pete walked out with my purse. "You forgot this."

"Thanks. Sorry. I can't believe I sang that song right after the guy I just broke up with was murdered. People will think I did it. Or that I'm insane," I warned.

"It's okay. I asked about the song. I thought you needed to cheer up a bit." Pete said.

I clutched my purse. "Why aren't you sadder?"

Pete shook his head. "I am, but I'm still in shock. Trying to patch things up with my brother and he goes and ends up dead."

"I'm sorry."

"You did nothing except what was right for you. Let me drive you home," he offered.

"You were drinking too," I said.

"I had one shot and a beer over an hour. I'm fine. I have a much bigger tolerance than you do. I saw, I'll be a gentleman," he insisted.

"Good. I have pepper spray and the sheriff's number in my cell phone," I warned.

He opened the door to the passenger side of his car. I slid in and felt better. Checking my phone, I had some messages and texts. But I couldn't read them once he started driving the car. Motion sickness was worst when a person was tipsy so I put the phone away and rolled down the window for some fresh air.

My eyes popped open when he was tried to help me out of the car.

"I'm good." I pushed his hands away.

We were parked by the RV. "Why are we over here?"

"I wasn't sure if you wanted to go into the house with your gran when you're a little drunk," he said.

"I'm not drunk. I could use a coffee, but I'm not breaking into the RV. Private property, even if it is parked on Gran's land," I replied.

"Okay, I just thought we might want to check out the inside. Those guys seem to be snake guys. Maybe they have one as a pet?" Pete suggested.

I couldn't rule it out. "Tell Gus and he'll check it out. I'm not breaking and entering. I'm not doing it with a stranger. You should go."

"You're going home?" he asked.

"None of your business where I go. Please leave. Thanks for the ride, but I'm good." I grabbed my purse and headed for the back porch. "I need some fresh air. Then I'll go to bed. You go."

Pete drove off and I felt sixteen years old and about to be grounded. But I'd never done this stuff at sixteen.

I wasn't the sweetest person when I'd had a few and I didn't trust myself around musicians when I was tipsy. I'd tried so hard to be good when I was younger that now little rebellions were sneaking out of me like when I was in college. That had to stop! I was grown. There was someone out there stuffing snakes into people's homes. As silly as it sounded, it could be deadly.

I looked around and stood up uneasily. There were snakes that belonged to the land, native and at home. Some were nice and ate rodents, but others could do a lot of damage with one bite. I quickly slipped through the back door and locked it. Duke started barking his head off. The one saving grace of a dog, if it saw a snake—inside the house or out on a walk—it'd let everyone know!

Chapter Five

I downed another cup of coffee as I preheated the ovens at the shop. Gran made sure to clang pans and bang the oven doors shut.

"Gran, please," I grumbled.

"I know you lost someone, but you're not some drunk. Hangovers are for college kids and morons," she lectured.

"I didn't drink that much. People were doing toasts to Luke, and his brother was there. After the snake in our backroom, I needed something for my nerves. What was I supposed to do?" I asked.

"Toast with water or Coke. It's the same sentiment," Gran scolded. "I called an exterminator to check back there. I've never seen any hint of a mouse, and we keep it clean, but checking is better. He can advise on putting down some snake-away or plugging up holes if he finds any."

"Sorry. I didn't want to keep feeling it all," I admitted. "Thanks for calling an exterminator. We'll have peace of mind then."

"You did nothing wrong. There's no guilt you need to drink away. Just be respectful and help solve the case. This town doesn't need more nonsense. I'll get these going. You eat something and have another cup of coffee," she instructed.

"I'm fine," I insisted.

"I'm not a feeble old woman. Not yet. I can put some dough in pans and set a timer. Once you've eaten, take down the chairs," she said.

"Fine." I went to the front and poured more coffee. A cinnamon roll seemed safe enough. I ate and checked the news on my phone.

As I started on the chairs, a tap on the door made me jump. I looked through the blinds. It was Pete.

I opened the door and let him in. "Hi. We're not open yet."

"I really need a decent cup of coffee. Do you mind?" He looked so lost.

"Sure. Motel coffee not cutting it?" I teased and let him in.

"I wanted to apologize for last night too. Luke always complained that I instigated things. You've got a great voice," Pete said.

"That's the last time I ever do that. You can't tell Gran."

"She'll know soon enough. Someone made a video," he advised.

"Damn." My headache returned.

"It's good. Relax. I bought the drinks and all that. It's my fault," Pete said.

"Really?" Gran's sharp disapproval came from behind the counters.

"Good morning, Mrs. Baxter. I was just apologizing to Belle here. I bought the drinks, I toasted my brother and I encouraged her. I'm sure she felt some odd sense of obligation to play along since I lost my brother," he pleaded.

"That wasn't her fault," Gran agreed.

"No, not at all. I don't know a lot of people in town and I was commiserating about my brother. She was being nice. A lot of people at the bar were. It's a very nice town and I'm sorry if I upset anyone." He helped with the chairs. "If I can make it up to you…"

"No, you're going through enough," I cut him off.

Gran nodded. "You have my condolences. I do hope you'll let us know about the arrangements for the funeral."

"Right. I talked to my parents. They called our old pastor who's a friend of the family. He'd like to do the service here at Luke's church, if that's okay," Pete offered.

"I'm sure the church board and mayor will allow it. Heavens, we'll need a new preacher. Well, God will provide. I do hope there will no more drowning your sorrows," Gran instructed.

"I think that phase of grieving is done. A bit of denial is hard to hold on to. He's gone and someone wanted that. Very scary," Pete replied.

"Is there anyone you knew of that would want Luke dead?" I asked.

"Not like that. There was a rival preacher when he was in bible college, but I'm pretty sure they forced those two to make peace. If pastors can't forgive each other, we're all going to Hell quick." Pete chuckled.

"Nice. You're no preacher," Gran replied.

"I could've been, but Luke got there first. I wanted to be my own man, not live in his shadow. Saving lives and putting out fires is good for the soul too. Keeps me in shape and the adrenaline up." Pete smiled.

I poured him a coffee. "Help yourself to breakfast. It's the least I can do, since you gave me a ride last night. Gran and I swung by the Buckle this morning and I got my car. No harm done."

"Anyone else?" Gran asked.

"I'm sorry?" Pete replied.

"Anyone else you think might have a grudge or bad blood with the pastor? Someone shoved that snake in there. Maybe they knew he was allergic, maybe they just wanted to terrify him," Gran pointed out.

"True, true. Let me think." He sipped his coffee.

"Okay, let me set up something before I forget." I went into my bag and pulled out a multiplug USB tower.

"What's that thing?" Gran asked as she opened the front door and flipped the sign.

"So people can charge their devices." The outlet crackled and sparked.

"I think it might be too much. You might need to update your electrical," Pete said.

"When we have the money," I grumbled.

"Sorry?" Pete asked.

"Nothing. Did you think of anyone else?" I put the charging tower back in my bag.

"He did mention a woman at a former church who hated him. She thought Luke had used her then dumped her. Not necessarily wrong, as they weren't officially dating. Then again, he mentioned he was seeing someone here in the choir."

"Me. I play piano for the choir." I couldn't believe he'd been cheating right under my nose.

"No, sorry, it wasn't you he was talking about. Maybe it was who he was seeing before. She was upset that he didn't propose to her and she thought that they were really serious. If you don't know who he was dating before…that's a little weird," Pete commented.

"He wasn't publicly dating anyone we knew of. But who cares?" Gran asked.

"Many love triangles are wrecked-tangles…but I had no idea if that's what he was doing. What if he was keeping her a secret? Like he was ashamed of her? That'd piss me off a lot. That could be a motive to scare him, at least. Maybe the snake in the house was a commentary…that he was a snake?" I suggested.

"Interesting theory," Pete agreed.

Gran came over and patted his hand. "If you need any help with the funeral, just let us know."

"Thanks. I guess I should be going," Pete said.

I felt bad. He didn't know many people or really belong here, but he was here and was going to bury his brother. Just then Gus walked in.

"There's the little star," he teased.

"What?" Gran asked.

"Nothing. Pete, did you talk to Gus about this lady from the old church? I don't think I got her name. He might want to check her out."

Pete nodded and sat down with Gus.

"I'll get you a coffee," I offered.

Gran headed to the table as her four guys walked in, bright and early as always.

I got Gus his usual and refilled Pete's. People started to come in, so I headed back to the counter and helped Gran. We were busy for a good hour, but Gus was still chatting with the guys. Martha came in halfway through the rush and I hit the washroom.

Then I snuck over to Gus' table.

"Anything good?" I asked.

Gus shrugged. "Angie Lowell. Was in the choir at his old church. She shouldn't be hard to track down. Check on an alibi. Pete seemed more relaxed about it last night."

I sighed. "Drinking to manage grief. I can't blame him. I felt bad for dumping him before he got crushed to death—I had a few."

Gus smiled. "I heard you were great."

"Right." I blushed.

"No, I mean the choice of song wasn't appropriate for the evening. But for getting up there on a dare, you sang well. You should try it again sober," he suggested.

I shook my head. "You want Gran over here with a wooden spoon to whack you into next week?"

"No. What's the big deal?" he asked.

"Bad enough I was drinking. Singing in public? I'm trying to help my family reputation, not make a fool of myself."

"Luke didn't help your family's reputation," Gus said.

I shot him a look. "That's not why I dated him. I broke up with him because he wasn't right for me. We weren't that serious, but it's a shock."

"Any other suspects?" he asked.

"I don't think his brother would do it, but they didn't seem close either. Pete just dropped in without notice and Luke wasn't thrilled," I explained. Harry walked in and headed right for Martha. "I should get back and help."

Gus nodded.

I handled a couple other customers and refilled creamer and sugar. Martha and Harry flirted.

"You're very happy. You and the pastor didn't see eye-to-eye but don't be mean," Martha teased Harry.

"I'm not happy about that. I'm happy you're happy. Once all this funeral stuff is over, maybe we can go out on a real date?" he asked.

She smiled. "Sounds good."

"Great. I just hope we get a more tolerant new pastor," he said.

I stepped back. I was eavesdropping.

Gus walked up for a refill. "Tolerant?"

"Yeah, Pastor Luke told my brother some things that were pretty ignorant thinking. Small towns don't mean small-minded." Harry shook his head.

"About Larry?" Gus asked.

Harry cleared his throat. "Yeah, some people found out he was gay and have made comments. He goes to the pastor for support and he gets...not support. Then people complain when young people leave small towns for cities."

"You think it's the intolerance?" Gus asked.

"Sure. Belle went to college in Atlanta to get away. I can't blame her. She did nothing, but her parents' behavior gave her nothing but grief. My brother can't change who he is. She can't change her parents. I don't think Pastor Luke would have approved of either of them," Harry said.

"Luke wouldn't disapprove of Belle," Martha jumped in.

"Not her. If her parents were around, do you think they'd have dated?" Harry asked.

I shook my head. "No. I don't think he would've. But we weren't right for each other, so it doesn't matter. His job is to support his congregation and give advice. He should've been better to Larry. I remember Larry came up to him the night Luke brought Pete into the bar. Larry wanted to talk. I didn't realize so many people knew about Larry."

"I don't think he should hide, but it's up to him. Then again, small-town gossip can be cruel." Harry shook his head.

"No kidding. No man tells the truth about himself — only his neighbors do," I said.

"I have to go to work. I'll see you later, Martha. Have a nice day, everyone." Harry slipped through the crowd.

* * * *

At choir practice, a lot of the women were sniffling and looking lost. I didn't want to go in, but I had to. Some looked at me with pity, some as though I hadn't deserved him, and others as if I'd lost out on the best thing in the world.

It was funny how death changed the way the deceased was viewed. A lot of times, all their bad traits suddenly vanished and people only remembered the good things. That was fine if it was an accident or natural causes. With a possible murder, there had to be motives examined.

"Should we practice?" one lady asked.

"Are we even having a service on Sunday?" Megan asked.

"His brother Pete said they'd have the funeral here with a guest pastor. I suppose we could brush up on funeral-appropriate songs," I suggested.

We barely got through *Amazing Grace* and a couple of the women broke down. I felt awful that I wasn't one of them, but I couldn't force it. I wasn't going to be fake.

I studied the women who were most hurt. A couple were giving me dirty looks off and on. Some were putting on an act. They had to put on a show — it was just how they acted. But how could I tell who'd been sneaking around with the pastor or previously dating him versus those who were just acting up?

"I'll grab some more tissues," I offered.

I headed for the big storage closet.

"Belle," the church secretary called.

"Yes, Mrs. Woodson?"

"You don't have to hide your tears, dear. And get some more tea bags while you're in there," she requested.

"Thanks, I will. You know, I think he was more interested in someone else. He was nice to me, but I don't think either of us felt any spark. It's just a horrible shame this happened and he never got to give the other relationship a real try." I hoped that threw enough guilt off me for the moment.

I went into the storeroom and grabbed a box of tissues, and when I went looking for the tea, I nudged a pile of blankets with my foot.

Then the blankets moved and made a noise.

"Snake!" I screamed and ran out of the room like I was five years old.

"Snake?" Mrs. Woodson looked in.

"No, I'm sorry. I'm not a snake." A man in boxers and an old T-shirt stumbled out. "I was asleep. I've been staying in there."

The women all looked at each other in shock. Then they looked at Mrs. Woodson.

"I had no idea," the secretary insisted.

"Pastor Luke knew, though. He said it was okay," the guy insisted.

"Really? Did you know him?" Mrs. Woodson asked.

"No, well, yes, before. I fell on hard times. I used to have a church of my own. We had a scandal. People were stealing money. I got all the blame. I've been trying to start over, but I'm not qualified for much else." The guy looked disoriented.

Glancing around, I saw most of us were shocked. Only Megan didn't seem scared.

"Why was he letting you stay here and not with him at his house?" I asked.

"I didn't want to be a problem or an object of pity. I was trying to get things together. I'm too young for social security or Medicare, probably too old to rebuild my reputation." He leaned on the wall. "I had some medical issues too. I got through that but was out of options."

"The pastor was very kind, but I wish he would've let me know. If I'd have found you, I'd have had a heart attack," Mrs. Woodson said.

"How do we know it's true?" another woman asked.

I grabbed my cell phone. "I'm texting the sheriff. He can sort out his story. I think we should cancel practice for today."

"You're not leaving me alone with him?" Mrs. Woodson asked.

"No, I'll wait with you. The sheriff is on his way." I checked my messages. "What's your name, Pastor?"

"Jeff Johnson," he replied.

"And where was your church?" I asked.

"Chattanooga, Tennessee."

I nodded and plugged the information into Google. "One eyewitness is better than ten hearsays."

The search was very productive, but I was going to wait for Gus.

Chapter Six

Gus arrived and Mrs. Woodson, a widow who was tall but very frail, relaxed and sighed in relief. "I'm so glad you're here, Sheriff. I had no idea there was someone living in the closet."

"It's okay, Mrs. Woodson. You can go back to the office and I'll stop by on my way out. Have some water or coffee. Sit down." Gus steered her out of the room.

Jeff had put on pants and a sweater, which made me more comfortable. I sat at the piano in the rehearsal room. Jeff paced the room barefoot.

Gus came back and cleared his throat.

"Sheriff, Jeff Johnson. He's been staying in that closet. Says he had Luke's permission," I said.

"He never told you?" Gus asked.

"Nope. And this isn't just a random homeless guy either. They have a history. Should I leave you two alone?" I asked.

"You can stay. I'd like to meet more people. Luke was ashamed of me, but I've paid my debts and made my peace with my mistakes. I want to rebuild my life and reputation," Jeff explained.

"Do you have ID?" Gus asked.

Jeff dug out a wallet from his pants and handed over his license. "I don't have warrants, but I do have a record a ways back."

"You're Belle, the girlfriend?" Jeff asked.

"I was. We broke up. Why stay here and not his house?" I asked.

"He didn't want to upset anyone. Like you, Belle. Or the congregation. He was helping me with his own money and I just crashed there. I was looking for a church or work. Luke was helping, but he didn't want people to judge me or think he was using their donations to pay my way," Jeff said.

"How can you get work if no one knows you're here?" I asked.

Jeff chuckled. "I was getting over a chest cold and he told me to focus on being healthy. I helped him with some sermons. He needed some advice."

I shared a look with Gus.

Gus nodded. "I see. He took advice from a homeless guy who he let sleep on the floor in a closet? Any chance you had a grudge against him?"

Jeff laughed. "No. Luke was always out of step with what people expected of him. He was harder on some people than others. The young man had some gifts, but he was still immature in many ways. An impressive preacher who saw potential in Luke helped him onto the fast track. They gave him chances most young wannabes never got. That's why you had such a young pastor. His next move was Nashville and a much bigger church."

"Sounds like a good deal. What was out of step?" Gus asked.

"Luke's beliefs were bit more conservative than the trajectory he's on. This is a nice solid Christian church. He's more angled conservative. Less tolerant. He was feeling conflicted," Jeff told us.

"Agreed," I said.

"What do you mean?" Gus asked.

"He didn't like me tending bar at Katie's. He wanted me to close the shop or hire someone else to work on Sundays. Seriously, Luke thought women should be homemakers and mothers—nothing more. It was creepy. Also, I think he's been giving some gay people not-great advice," I warned.

"I'm going to talk to Larry about that," Gus replied.

"Were you trying to get him to change churches?" I asked Jeff.

Jeff nodded. "I told him he needed the right congregation. He'd been keeping things general and open, so most people liked him here. They didn't see his real opinions. But some of the couples he was counseling saw it. He couldn't keep it up forever."

"He talked to you about that?" I asked.

"In confidence. But he's dead. I don't know who he offended or upset. Some of the wives he was counseling were pissed. The old-fashioned opinions don't fly in modern congregations. You need old-fashioned hardcore bible fire-and-brimstone groups, but those on his level tend to be smaller," Jeff advised.

"Do you know Pete?" I asked.

"Sure." Jeff cracked his knuckles. "He wanted to be a preacher too, I think. But his brother got tapped. Not by me. I wasn't anything special to bring someone along. They came to the church where I was training.

Luke always took the hard line, the strict interpretations. Pete was more open to modern interpretations."

Gus scratched his chin. "Give me an example."

"He never drank alcohol that I saw. Some churches interpret Jesus turning water to wine as grape juice. Or the thing about women being obedient to their husbands as frozen in time," I explained.

"That would not go over well in marriage counseling," Jeff pointed out.

"That pisses off the wives. I don't see many women handling a four-foot python, but maybe that's sexist?" Gus wondered.

I shivered. "I wouldn't touch one of those snakes, venomous or not, but it doesn't require any specialized man parts to do it."

"Most people feel that way. But some people have odd pets," Jeff agreed.

"You ever handle snakes?" I asked.

Jeff shook his head. "Those churches are very fringe. Talking in tongues is one thing but using venomous snakes? Trusting God is one thing, but testing Him? I'll go on faith."

"Did he tell you about anyone that he was afraid of or thought hated him? Was anyone out to get him?" I asked Jeff.

Leaning on the wall, Jeff sighed. "Not that he said. I know he pissed off a few people at his last church. That's why he didn't get into a bigger one in the city yet. He had to prove he could keep on message and not veer off into the wrong lane."

"Anyone here? They'd need to know his schedule and where he lived," Gus pointed out.

"Not that I know of. The secretary seemed to like him. The choir ladies never talked badly behind his back. I can hear a lot in there. Some of the ladies thought he could do better than Belle, but he never said that. I'd say he gave someone private counseling and it sent them down a dark path. Or someone from his life before," Jeff offered. "But I don't know all of his life here. He kept himself compartmentalized."

"Clearly. Okay, we can't leave you here. Do you have anywhere else you can stay?" Gus asked.

Jeff shook his head. "I can move on, but I'm guessing you're not going to let that happen."

"I'm going to detain you until I run you for any warrants, issues or anything. That'll let you stay in our holding cell. Food, showers and TV. We can only do that for so long without charging you, but if you're still a person of interest, we can put you up at the motel unless one of the deputies will let you stay at their home — under their watch," Gus explained.

"I'm not running. Motel sounds nice. How do you know I wouldn't take off?" Jeff asked.

Gus laughed. "We've got ankle bracelets that track people. Just to be sure, you're not on parole? That generally limits where you can legally travel."

Jeff crossed his heart. "I served my time. I got a lot of debt, but who doesn't?"

"You're okay with being detained?" Gus asked.

"If it helps solve a murder? Sure. Food and TV are good. Luke got me food, but it's been a rough couple of days wondering how to introduce myself." Jeff nodded. "I'll grab my things."

"Pete is staying at the motel. I'm sure he'd like to see you. You're welcome to Baxter's Jams and More for coffee and pastries whenever. On the house. If you need anything, just let me know," I offered.

Jeff smiled. "Luke missed out. But you're better off. Marriage is very tricky. Falling in love is easy, but forever—that takes partnership and communication. Luke liked people to listen, not talk back."

"We'd never have made it." I chuckled. "May he rest in peace."

"Come on, Mr. Johnson, let's get your stuff. Do you have any weapons?"

"A couple pocket knives, but that's it." Jeff led the way.

"Thanks, Gus. I'm going to check on Gran at the shop. Tell Mrs. Woodson so she can lock up when you go," I explained.

"I'll catch up with you later," Gus called.

"Okay." I checked my messages. "Gran has Pete there. We need to work on the funeral plans."

"See you there in a bit," he called.

* * * *

I arrived back at the shop to find it without power.

"We're working on it," Milan said.

"What happened?" I asked.

"The boys wanted to put up your charging tower thing. A bunch of teenagers came in and wanted to charge their phones and tablets. Then *poof*. We need to get the electrical box fixed." Gran wagged a finger.

"Necessity sharpens industry. We need a handyman who won't charge an arm and a leg," I agreed. "But for now, we need power."

"Relax. Everyone paid for their stuff. If they didn't have cash, I put them on an account for now." Gran waved it off like it was nothing.

"We're not *Little House on the Prairie*, Gran. We need electricity." I pulled the plug from the wall. "Try it again please, Milan."

They flipped something and the lights came back on.

The men came out, congratulating each other. Gran fawned over them for a few minutes

"Now, back to the funeral plans." Gran sat down in a corner with Pete.

"Sorry, I didn't see you there," I said to Pete.

"No problem. It's just sad, picking hymns and readings," he replied.

"I got the book from Mrs. Woodson," Gran whispered to me.

I nodded. "I'm going to get some coffee and I'll be right back."

I picked up a big hunk of corn bread while I was at it and joined them.

"When will your pastor friend arrive?" Gran asked.

"On the day of it. He has his own church to deal with. It's so hard to believe, it's crazy." Pete flipped pages in the book.

"Did you know about Jeff Johnson?" I asked.

"What about him?" Pete looked up. "He lost his church and had some issues. The guy kind of disappeared."

"He reappeared in the church storage room. Scared us to death," I informed him.

"You're kidding?" Pete asked.

"No, he's now at the police station with Gus. I'm not sure how long he's been in there, but he might need another friend going forward." I turned to Gran. "I told him he could come in for coffee and pastry on the house."

She leaned in. "Why is he under arrest?"

"He's not. Not under arrest, just detained until they make sure he has no warrants or whatever. Gus is being nice—food, washroom and a place to sleep. We can't just leave him living in the church. I don't know if he has a car or any money, but he's a stranger to us. People wouldn't feel safe with him in the church," I said.

Pete nodded. "If they release him, he can stay at the motel with me. I've got a room with two beds. He's a good guy. Not as crazy conservative as others."

"Yeah, Jeff gave Gus and me a quick crash course in tracks for the church. He said you were more moderate. Luke was hiding his conservative nature until he got into the big leagues or found a very conservative church to join." I frowned. "It's the bible belt. I'm sure he could've located a church to fit his views."

Pete shook his head. "Maybe, but they're still smaller, generally. Big churches have to keep women involved and valued enough to support the leadership. The young people need to be on board as well, or the mega churches won't work. There's a balance. Luke wants—wanted—the fame and the big screens. He wasn't good at playing the game of pretending to be on board with that balanced approach. He'd skew hard right and get the moderate people upset."

I folded my arms. "Some of those big churches are really conservative, though."

"Some. Not all. Not as conservative as he is. Luke was waiting for the right chance. That's why he kept sticking to small churches. If he screwed up or upset people, another small church would give him a chance.

If he failed on a huge platform, his career would be over." Pete sighed.

"Big dreams. Lots of people have them, but they aren't what they're cracked up to be. Small-town life, healthy family and pursuing what makes you happy—that's good enough for most people," Gran advised.

I nodded. "Anyway, I'm not sure what Mr. Johnson will do, but I wanted to tell you he's here."

Pete circled the hymns and readings. "No flowers. Donations to the church food pantry or their favorite charity is good."

"Did you meet with the funeral director? Pick out the coffin? We can find a suit," Gran offered.

"No, I'm going to have him cremated so I can just take him with me. Put him in the family plot back home. We'll do it all at the church. No graveside." Pete set down the pen firmly.

"And the reception?" I asked.

"We can't use his house. Still a crime scene," Pete replied.

"Do we know what happened to the snake?" I asked.

"I guess they checked it for chips or any other owner information. There was none," Pete said.

"I know—we'll do the food and such here," Gran suggested.

I shook my head. "Gran, that's going to be weird. We can do it at the church. One big event. Food and reception in the foyer and outside, weather permitting."

"No graveside—it'll be unconventional enough," Gran grumbled.

I smiled at Pete. "Most people around here go for traditional burial. I'm surprised the funeral home does cremation."

"It's a bit less expensive and he'd want his ashes buried with the family." Pete stood. "Done?"

"That's it. I'll let Mrs. Woodson know," Gran replied.

"Thank you, Mrs. Baxter. It feels very odd. Your kindness is very helpful."

Pete left quickly.

"What a weird situation to be in," I admitted.

Gran nodded. "But we must do something to say good-bye. Then the board will have to look for a new pastor."

"Great. More new people." My phone binged. The text message was from Gus.

"What is it?" Gran asked.

"Gus wants to meet for dinner away from town. Go over suspects and what we know," I explained.

"Another date?" Gran teased.

"No, let's hope it's a nice clearing of the air." I texted him back that I'd meet him there at six o'clock.

"I'll have dinner with the boys, then. They'll know a handyman who can work on the wiring. Upgrade the electrical. It's only when we try to add stuff."

"Have fun on your date," I teased.

She swatted my hand.

* * * *

I pulled up to the restaurant and Gus was there, waiting in his truck.

"Everything okay?" I asked as I hopped out.

He met me by the door. "Fine. If you like Chinese. I wasn't sure."

"Love it. I miss the city for things like this. Variety of food. Home cooking is the best, but sometimes you want to order pizza or Chinese." I walked while he held the door.

We got a booth and both of us went with the buffet to save time and interruptions. Once our water and iced teas arrived, we filled up our plates and settled in.

I took a little bit of all my favorites to see which of their versions I liked. Spicy was good, but every place was different.

"You like spicy," he teased.

"I do. Atlanta had so many options. Nashville is good too." I smiled.

"I know this is weird, but you were the last one to see Luke and probably the closest person to him," he said.

I frowned. "Pete informed me that his brother might've been seeing someone else too."

"You mean before at his prior church?" Gus asked.

I sampled the Empress chicken and frowned. "Too much onion. Sorry, no, Pete said he was seeing someone else here. Someone in the choir."

"You don't like onion?" he asked.

"Not when it's the only flavor I'm tasting. The orange chicken is good. General's chicken is very good. How's yours?"

"Good. Beef with broccoli is my go-to."

"You and Dina came here?" I asked.

He grimaced and tried to hide it with a grin. "We did occasionally. Are you ready to hear the truth?"

"You said you broke up with her and didn't bother to demand the ring back. She was trying to keep her claws in you even though she's the one who was seeing other people?"

"More or less," he agreed.

"What's the more part of that answer?"

"I tried ending it a few times. She always had a crisis where I felt bad and stuck by her. A family member died, she had a pregnancy scare or she got fired. Finally, I ended it and meant it." He gestured for emphasis.

"She thought you were crying wolf again. Well, she found another guy, which is good. But you don't want to play games. It only makes it worse."

"With you?" he asked.

"With any woman. She's going to cry, scream and make it hell every time. If you're serious, do it once and it's done. Easier on both of you. Some women are so clingy. I never want to be that," I insisted.

"You could never be," he said.

I dunked my egg roll in duck sauce. "Then other ladies say I'm too cold and independent. Men don't want someone who doesn't need them."

He chuckled. "Sounds like my grandma warning me about those career girls who just want to date man after man and never settle down. They don't want to cook, clean or raise babies."

I nearly choked on my rice and took a long drink of water. "Exactly. Who wants to clean house? I mean, it's necessary, but few people love it. The point is, women's work and their role in the family got devalued because we weren't getting paid. Men made the money so they had the power. If you married a good guy, you'd be okay, but if you married a jerk or someone who liked that control…you could be stuck in a horrible situation. Gran got lucky, but it's too much of a gamble. Now you have to pay for daycare and so on or do it yourself."

"Because now women work too," he added.

"You think that's a bad thing? Have you heard about Sally and Ed?"

Gus cleared his throat. "I can't talk about cases."

"Oh, so she came to you?" I asked. "She's been gone for weeks now, so I don't think she'd care if we talked. I'm not telling Ed a thing."

"I saw her marks. She works at the grocery store, I asked. She claimed it was nothing. I went by the house, social call to Ed. He didn't care for it. I went by again when Ed was on a haul. She refused to press charges. Even refused to say he'd hit her so I could bring him in. I can't force her, and without seeing him do it or her word that he had, I can't initiate the charges unless I see the assault," Gus explained.

"I know. I appreciate your trying to help. She's been gone for two weeks. Someone helped her. And she can get a job and a credit card and all that stuff in her own name. I know people long for the good old days when life was simpler, people stayed married and so on...but that's always with a happy couple that's good to each other. Plus, us sad spinsters deserve equal pay." I tried the sweet and sour chicken. "That sauce is a bit too tomato-heavy for me."

"Picky eater," he teased.

"No, I'm just sampling to see what I like and don't. Means I'm willing to try new things. Second round, I'll get my favorites only."

"That's a good strategy. I like it. What happened with the pastor?" Gus asked.

I smiled. "You've heard, I'm sure. I dumped him very loudly in an Italian restaurant. He wanted an old-fashioned pastor's wife to be at his and the church's beck and call 24/7. Me helping out at the bar was somehow reflecting badly on him. Working at the shop on a Sunday too. I don't think he liked the band having their RV parked on the property, but he couldn't say anything about that because Gran owns the land. Some men want to be the boss without conversation or question. It wasn't going to work, so I ended it. He was so stunned, like I had to be out of my mind."

"He didn't harass you?" Gus asked.

"No, I don't think he'd want to take the chance people might overhear or see anything more. He always wanted to look like he had the answers. He was way more conservative than he let on in public or in his sermons," I warned Gus.

Nodding, Gus reached for his water. "He never said anything to me, but everyone has secrets. The deputies have talked to a few people who have a lot of pets — reptiles of various kinds. So far no one is missing or claims to have owned a Burmese python."

"I've never heard of anyone owning a snake around here. Kids catch them or something, but a stray python… That's not normal. I know sometimes guys will go hunting when the rattlers are getting too close or too thick and putting people off. Sometimes cattle and horses are getting bitten, so they do a roundup, but it's been a while," I explained.

"This snake will have to be euthanized. It's not native and unless someone claims it as their pet, we can't let it live. Animal Control has it now, but even with proper feeding, it's a fairly aggressive snake. Doesn't seem like someone's pet." He leaned in.

I smiled.

"What? Miss me?" he teased.

"You got sauce on your cuff." I pointed.

He laughed and lifted his wrist. "Sauce on everything." He wiped it off.

"I missed you. You're different. Not feeling judged by you is nice. But your complicated recent past—I'm not going to be the other woman."

Gus sighed. "It's not like that. She and I are done. Not every woman out there is independent like you."

"Men always seem to like the clingy ones, until they don't. I'm not going to play in some weird tug-of-war over a man. I'd rather be alone with my shop and have people feeling sorry for the spinster than make a fool of myself," I said.

"Like you'd be a spinster." He laughed.

"It's possible. Not needing a man doesn't mean I don't want one. I'm not good at being fake or playing games like your ex or Lurlene. Why do men like to play the knight in shining armor?" I asked.

"Society tells us to be the hero. My job is to help people, all the people. I know this is difficult, but life is complicated. I can't control her. You can't control any of your ex-boyfriends. If one showed up to bug you, I'd have to deal with it," he agreed.

"If I had one that obsessively bad and recent, I'd tell you about it before we got involved. I guess that's the loophole. We weren't really involved before. We were solving a murder, not really dating. Just seems like such a coincidence," I explained.

"Dina has higher hopes than a sheriff, trust me. I thought she just had a rough childhood and needed stability, but she's a climber. Wanted to meet politicians and businessmen that a sheriff got to know. She'll be the governor one day, or his wife," Gus replied.

I shook my head. "Is that your type? Girls who need stability and saving?"

Gus sighed. "That's not what I meant. If you want to disqualify me, you don't need a reason. Tell me you're not interested and I'll leave you alone, except for murder stuff and getting coffee at the shop."

"I don't know you well enough to know one way or the other yet. I'm not trying to judge you by your past, but what else is there? I don't want people judging me by my parents' behavior, but they do. My grandpa bought a bunch of land on the cheaper side of town. He figured he wasn't going to farm it, so more land is better than rich soil. People judge each other for stupid things."

"They do. They also murder each other for stupid reasons. Passion, money, revenge, lust, authority or fear. Money and authority don't seem likely for motives here. The others are possible, but it wasn't impulsive. They planted a snake and waited. The intent might not have been murder, which makes this case trickier," he said.

"Do you believe Jeff?"

Gus sighed. "No warrants in the state. We're checking with others. Making sure he's safe to release. It's just a big coincidence. It happens when his brother is in town and he's hiding an old friend. Why not ask someone to put him up? If Luke really believed Jeff was harmless…why not introduce you?"

"I have no idea. Maybe he was ashamed of the connection? That's what I don't get. If he wanted to be moving up, he should've asked out Lurlene. Her family owns a business, she's in beauty school and she'd love to be the pastor's wife with all of that responsibility and power," I grumbled.

"You don't?"

"No. I see the reality that it's all free work. If you have a lot of money, it's cool. I'm all for charity, but the pastor is paid. Why is the wife expected to do a ton of work for nothing?"

Gus shook his head. "I have no idea. But you're not a pastor's wife."

"No?" I tilted my head. "I'm a career girl with a bakery shop who moonlights as a bartender for her friend's bar."

"Maybe. You can be whatever you want." He stood. "Round two, where I'll probably get something else on my shirt."

"Oh, I did think of one thing that was weird." I stood and followed him to the buffet.

"What's that?" He grabbed a new plate and handed me one.

"Thanks. When we saw Jeff in the storage closet. Everyone was scared and shocked, even Mrs. Woodson. But Megan didn't seem to be shocked by the news. I'm not saying she knew he was there, but it didn't faze her at all. That's odd," I remarked.

"It is." He filled his plate.

I went for the General's chicken and white rice and egg rolls. "I wonder if they deliver?"

"To our neck of the woods? No."

"What do you mean *our* neck of the woods?" I asked.

He smiled. "I may have put an offer in on that ranch next door."

"Ranch?" I scoffed. To one side of our property was a quiet couple who had horses. The other side was unoccupied except for the doublewide the couple had left behind. "The Conners moved a year ago, according to Gran."

"Lots of land for cheap. I can build the house I want and live in that trailer until then. Seems like the perfect set up, but the neighbors do have this RV with a band on their property. I hope it's not too noisy," he teased.

"You're not serious."

"We'll see." He winked at me.

I shrugged it off and forced myself not to smile like a fool. "You can't control your neighbors, now, can you? Although good fences make good neighbors, but that's a costly fence to erect."

Chapter Seven

The next evening, Gran and I were working on apple pies and peach cobbler.

"I don't know how they haven't found the owner of that snake by now," Gran said.

I smiled. "Do you want them to go house to house and search?"

"Wouldn't hurt. But I suppose people wouldn't like it."

"I agree." I rolled out more crust. "I told Gus what I know, but no help, apparently."

Gran put some pies in the oven. "You know, trucks come and go from all over. Snakes could've gotten on a truck in Florida and ended up here. It might be an accident."

I sighed. "A few snakes make it here, sure. But getting into a private home? It's so random. You'd think it'd manage to get into a store or something easier. Fewer steps, more traffic. But that might keep them away. I don't know much about snakes, but Luke was a door locker. He didn't leave things open, even his back door. Someone probably had to put it inside."

"I think I'll call Gus," she said.

"Why?" I asked.

"We can discuss the case. But put the casserole in the oven," she instructed.

"You want him over for dinner," I concluded.

Gran smiled. "Everyone has to eat, Annabelle."

My full first name, no arguments needed. I put the casserole in the oven and took the fancy yeast rolls out of the freezer. "Should I make a salad?"

She waved me off as she spoke with Gus. The woman wasn't a matchmaker, but she wasn't going to ignore something if she wanted it.

I worked on a Caesar salad, for something a bit different.

"He'll be here in half an hour," she informed me.

I loaded the fridge with premade pies to bake later and a couple of cobbler pans.

Gran wiped down the table then set up the dough for baking. When she took off her apron, I noticed her hand was a bit shaky.

"You feeling okay?" I asked.

"Sure. You should change. You're covered in flour. The way to a man's heart is through his stomach, but he doesn't need to see the mess. Apron or not, you always get messy when you're baking," she said with a smile.

I looked down. "Okay. Don't let the dog get in the food."

She gave me a thumbs up then checked her hair in the reflection of the window.

Rolling my eyes, I went into my bedroom and changed. I pulled on cowboy boots and a summer dress with little yellow flowers on it. Brushing out my hair, I tried to make it look nice loose. Finally, I gave up and pulled it back with a ribbon. I touched up my makeup and added a tiny bit of perfume.

All that work and I was sure he'd get back with Dina one day. Not that he'd said anything like that during our dinner, but I knew girls like her. She knew a good guy when she saw one and wanted to sink her claws in. Goofing things up could cost her time and she'd have to try harder to get him back.

Life had never handed me easy passes like some people got. I wasn't going to fall into the trap of thinking I was going to get one now — no matter how much Gran tried to help.

I went out and buttered the rolls before I put them in the oven. When I started to set the table, I realized how rarely we had company. If Gus bought the place next door, this might become a habit.

No way in hell was I telling Gran about that until it was a sure thing. She'd never let up about it.

"You okay, dear?" Gran asked.

I looked up. "Sure. Why?"

"You're standing there holding the silverware like you've forgotten how to set a table," she teased.

"Just lost in thought. Murders make me overthink." I set the table and made sure we had beer to offer Gus as well as Coke and iced tea.

Gran must've met Gus at the door, because I never heard a doorbell. When I turned, he was in the kitchen.

"Hi, would you like something to drink?" I offered.

"Sweet tea?" he asked.

"House wine of the south. I don't like mine super sweet, so I won't be offended if you add sugar." I gestured to the table as I poured him a glass.

I had some myself and filled Gran's glass. "Dinner is almost ready. We have salad."

"I didn't expect dinner. I thought I was just dropping by to discuss the case," he explained.

"A southern woman missing an attempt to feed people? Gran would never forgive herself," I teased.

The oven dinged. "Rolls," Gran announced.

I got them and checked on the casserole. "Almost done. Gran, come have salad."

She had worked her way around to the mud room. "Feeding Duke, then I'll let him out to run. It's nice and cool out."

"You need to eat," I informed her.

"Caesar salad, fancy. Showing off your cooking?" he teased.

"I've been baking so much, it's nice to do something different once in a while. Dinner is just Gran's hamburger and spiral noodle casserole. It was my favorite as a kid." I smiled.

"I can't wait to try it."

"It's basically spaghetti with a little cheese on top. Very tomato saucy and all that. I should've put in garlic bread, really." I sat down and dished out salad. "Any progress?"

Gran strolled in and washed her hands. "Duke is chasing geese."

I served her some salad and a roll. "I was just asking Gus about the case."

"Oh yes. I wondered about trucks. Couldn't it have just happened to be on a truck?" Gran stabbed her salad.

I pulled out the casserole and tested the center to make sure it was fully hot, then returned it to the oven to keep it warm.

"I suppose it's possible. I can check with the local truckers who own their rigs. Deliveries to stores like the grocery store...they'd be in and out—if the snake was found there, it might be possible, but for it to slither all the way to the pastor's house? I doubt we'd find any real evidence unless we find other snakes. I'm afraid I'm going to have to put more effort into the people around him than the accidental options."

"If it was a rattlesnake or a cottonmouth, that'd be a lot more likely to find a crack in the foundation or get trapped in the garage by accident," I reasoned.

"Two murders too close to each other. It's upsetting, Belle," Gran admitted.

I patted her arm. "I know. I don't get it either, but they're not connected. It's not a serial killer or anything like that."

Gus nodded. "Yes, these seem to be highly personal. The last one certainly was. There's no danger to anyone else."

"Is Belle in danger?" Gran sniffed.

"No, whoever did this was after Luke. Even with the snake in the back of your shop, that's likely a prank or a coincidence. We don't know of anything Luke's done that's bad. Belle doesn't. It's probably a grudge from years ago. Things pop up. His brother showing up right around that time, that still makes me wonder." Gus took a drink of tea.

"I haven't seen anything mean or cruel from Pete," Gran replied.

I pulled the casserole out and set it on the table. "I agree, but maybe he thought he'd forgiven his brother and let it all go, but something in his life changed and he had to hash it out. Or he needed to act out. We can't always know what makes people do what they do, but

I don't think we're in any danger. Gus will find the killer. And maybe it'll turn out they just wanted to scare him or send a message and Luke tried to handle the snake instead of running or calling Animal Control."

"He doesn't strike me as a hero." Gran dished out her casserole.

"The snake is very aggressive. Animal Control is ready to destroy it when we don't need it as evidence any longer," Gus said.

We all ate, and Gran seemed to calm down.

"This is wonderful," Gus complimented.

"Belle's favorite since she was little." Gran smiled. "Have some more. I make it all the time. Easy and good for you."

"Jeff and Pete are the two new equations in town," I analyzed.

"Jeff has a record, but nothing active. He has debts and lost most everything. Pete has a job, an apartment and no warrants. He was a bit wild in college, but nothing surprising. Neither have any warrants. I don't know why either would want Luke dead." Gus shrugged.

"You'll figure it out. Makes me feel safe to have someone who cares about everyone," Gran said. "More casserole?"

I offered more rolls as well. I smiled at Gran then locked eyes with Gus. Suddenly it felt like I was drinking wine and not iced tea. "I'm sure he has work to do. We can't keep him here all night."

Gran frowned. "I didn't make a dessert. But we could have one of the apple pies that was for tomorrow."

"Oh no, I'm stuffed. I was going to head to the Buckle and chat with people. That's why I'm not in uniform. People are more open when they think you're off duty." He smiled.

"You should take Belle, then it looks more like a date. Undercover." Gran winked.

I laughed. "You're as subtle as a cat in heat, Gran."

"I went through the change many years ago, thank you. You're the one who needs to get out there before all your eggs have hatched or been lost. Anyway, go solve a murder so you can have personal lives."

Gus sighed. "I won't object to help."

"Good. Go. I'm going to put the leftovers away and have some ice cream in front of the TV." She went to the back and let the dog in. "Duke will keep me company and safe."

I turned off the ovens and brought down the containers so she could reach everything easily. "I'll wash the dishes later."

"I can wash my own dishes, girl. Git!" Gran scolded.

* * * *

At the bar, we sat on the stools. A small table would look too much like a date and people might leave us alone. Katie was behind the bar and Martha was waiting tables.

It felt like we were on display. I was dating before my ex was buried—but I'd broken up with him. Or was there a proper grieving time?

Why can I never stay in the normal lanes? I always have to be the odd one out.

Things weren't exactly somber at the bar. There was no live music, but the jukebox played mostly slow songs and couples danced.

Katie walked up to us with a little twinkle in her eye. "What'll it be?"

"Beer for me. Belle?" Gus asked.

I smiled. "Rum and Diet Coke with lime, thanks."

Gus didn't order for me or give me a look when I ordered a drink. What had I been thinking with Luke? I knew what...that I hadn't thought he was as conservative as he'd turned out to be. That didn't mean Gus was Mr. Right, either. I had to slow down and be careful.

Martha hustled up with an order.

"Hey, Belle. Hey, Sheriff," Martha greeted. "Did you hear about today at the store?"

"Hi. What happened?" I asked.

"Evening. I actually wanted to ask you a few questions, but go ahead with your story first," Gus said.

Martha frowned. "Sure. Well, it's probably just a coincidence like it was at the back of the Preserve Shop...but usually they aren't alive."

"Martha, what? Another snake?" I asked.

She nodded. "Nasty cottonmouth this time. It's been pretty dry lately so they go looking for water. Occasionally, we do find the odd dead snake in the warehouse. They sneak in to cool off and get run over by a forklift or something. But someone found this one back when they were restocking the refrigerated section."

"In the store part?" Gus asked.

"No, by the milk and stuff you stock from behind. No customers were in any danger. They called Animal Control and it was safely removed, but the bosses were all worried. Everyone was checking under everything—they had stock boys sweeping the aisles instead to make sure nothing else was found," Martha said.

"Didn't call us," Gus said.

"It's not a *crime* crime. We're all seeing links where none exist. She said snakes are found back there. Usually dead, but one got lucky and stayed hidden in the right pallet to get to the front." I shrugged it off.

"Still, with the snake activity lately, I'd appreciate a call." Gus shot a look at Martha.

"I told my mom, but the owners were afraid of bad press. It's the only grocery store in town. People can't be afraid to go in there. I know there's an open field behind the store and when it's rainy, that little creek forms, but people get panicky." Martha explained.

"Especially when there's a possible murder in town. Maybe someone's goofing off. Planting dangerous snakes in public areas is endangering people, so that's my business," Gus reminded her.

"That's why I'm telling you. But please don't tell Momma you heard it from me," Martha warned.

"Fair enough," Gus agreed.

Martha smiled. "Thank you. Now what did you want to ask me about, Sheriff?"

"Pastor Luke. Your mom said he was pretty routine about his shopping. Mondays, and he always went to your lane if you were working," he recounted.

Martha nodded. "I guess so. Monday mornings isn't our busiest time, so we don't have a ton of lanes open."

"But he never showed up the Monday before his body was found?" Gus asked.

"Nope. Not that I remember. But I knew from here that his brother had dropped into town, so I figured his schedule would be off. Out-of-town guests mean more meals out and things are different," Martha remarked.

"Very true. In the last few weeks before his death, did you notice any changes in his habits? What he bought or how much of it?" Gus asked.

Martha wiped her hands on her half apron then used the hand sanitizer she knew was right behind the bar. "Actually, I did. The week before, I commented that he'd bought a few duplicates and extras. His bill was more than normal. He said something about donating to the pantry and didn't want people to make a big deal about it. But I'd guess it was that guy living in the church."

"You heard already?" Gus asked.

"The whole town hears things pretty quickly. Especially when you work here, the grocery store or Belle's shop. When I work at all those places, I hear it all more than once." She smiled.

Katie put the final glass on Martha's tray. "Order's ready. And you two need to take that class to get certified with the state for serving alcohol, or the sheriff might have to detain you next time."

"Dang it, I meant to look that up. I'll drop these off and we'll set that up. Be right back," Martha called.

I pulled out my phone and searched for the class. "Nashville. Of course," I replied.

"That's a nothing class. You could sleep through it," Gus teased.

"Said the sheriff. I'm not getting Katie in any trouble. It's only three evenings and the test."

Gus turned to Katie. "Any info flowing about the pastor? Was he ever here drowning his sorrows?"

Katie shook her head. "Only came into the bar with Belle or if someone had called him to come help. Usually that meant dragging home someone who shouldn't be drinking or taking someone to an AA meeting. He wasn't fond of drinking."

"Or me working here," I added.

Katie sighed. "Plenty of fish in the sea."

"It just don't make a lick of sense. Why hide Jeff in the church? There are plenty of shelters in Nashville. That'd have to be more comfortable than sleeping in the closet on a pile of blankets. Was he going to try to bring Jeff on as an associate pastor but wanted to see if Jeff was sober and clean? Or wanted to make sure he wasn't stealing or something? It doesn't add up," I insisted.

Gus sipped his beer. "Jeff said he and Luke hadn't made any firm plans. Jeff has been in touch with a couple of cousins out in Knoxville. He might have a place to stay there. He said he turned up on Luke's door after a message on Facebook. He gave him more notice that Pete did."

"Luke was charitable. He paid off a few bar tabs of people who got sober and stayed that way," Katie added.

"Cutting into your business?" I teased.

She chuckled. "You know I'm the first person to cut someone off and send them to AA if they have a problem. But I can't force them to stop drinking at home or go to meetings. I can't stop them from going to another bar. Plenty of people around here like a little drink with their socializing and no one gets hurt. I appreciate him paying. Writing off a tab where I know they drank and I'm not getting paid hurts the business."

I grumbled. "Not fair. Luke had good points."

Martha rushed back. "Did you find it?"

I showed her my phone. "Yep, there's one next week, or we have to wait three weeks. Fill it out."

She got on her phone and we both filled out the form. "Submit."

"Done."

We waited and got the 'enrolled' message.

"Good, we both got in. I'll chip in for gas if you'll drive," Martha offered.

"Don't worry about it. I'll drive." I waved it off.

"Your truck looks pretty beat up," Gus teased.

"It's fine. Held together by will and luck. If we have any car trouble, I know who to call." I grinned at him.

Martha and Katie shared a look.

"I saw that," I warned them.

"It's not you two," Martha whispered.

"Hey, Lurlene, what are you drinking?" Katie asked.

"Long Island, please." Lurlene sat down on the next free stool.

"Miss Lurlene, it will please you to know that Belle and I are all signed up for the proper class. We will be official in plenty of time for it to be all legal." Martha showed her the phone.

"Good, you can be officially trained to serve people. Go do it." Lurlene dismissed her.

Martha walked off and wouldn't look at anyone.

"That was nasty even for you," I shot at Lurlene.

"Who cares? I teased her once about something and she's worried. More of a Goody Two-shoes than you. But she has two kids. But she was married when she had them. You're still worse." Lurlene shot me a look.

"Were you drinking at home?" I asked.

"My business. I didn't drive here. Lyft," Lurlene said to Gus. Then she glared back at me. "You get whatever you want. Everyone, feel sorry for Belle because her parents ran off."

"Feel sorry? I don't want your pity," I informed her.

"But you always got it. If I wanted to give it or not." Lurlene shrugged.

"What? You know envy shoots at others but hits itself," I warned.

"Envy? God strike me dead if I ever really envied you. You got invited to things by all the kids — you got treated like you were normal because you weren't. Your parents ran off on you. Kids don't get it. Who doesn't have parents? I asked my mom, 'Did Belle's parents die in a car crash?' and she said no. They ran off. How bad of a kid do you have to be for your parents to run off?" Lurlene scoffed.

"That's enough," Gus warned.

"And you got this one back in a snap. He's better for you. You'd never make it as a pastor's wife. Why couldn't you just leave him for someone else? Instead he got involved with you and that just cursed him. You're a curse, Belle Baxter. The former sheriff tried to cut you a break and he ended up dead. Pastor Luke tried to help you and now he's dead too," Lurlene said.

"You sound like you're thirteen and I'm not invited to your sleepover, again," I replied.

Lurlene laughed. "My mom and all the other girls thought you were invited and you had to stay home because you had awful cramps. Boys knew all about it too."

I shook my head. "Keep living in the past, Lurlene. It's like your best days are all behind you."

"Duh, high school was the best. Beauty school is fun too, but prom queen and not having to work? Life was better. Don't fool yourself into thinking it gets better in a stupid small town." Lurlene sucked down half of her drink in seconds.

"Easy," Katie warned.

"Cut me off and I'll go home and drink more. I'm trying to spread the wealth. Make you some money. No one appreciates my patronage," Lurlene complained.

I turned to Gus. "Why don't you try to talk to Katie's brothers? They'll be working the door now. Luke was advising Larry a bit, but I'm not sure how it went."

"Okay, holler if you need me." He took his beer and headed for the door.

"See, you ran off the sheriff too. You'll screw it up, whatever happens," Lurlene taunted.

"That's why I'm no competition for you. Luke probably knew you were too good for him." I wiped my hands on the bar towel.

"What?" She squinted at me and put both hands flat on the bar like she was steadying herself.

Being the underdog, I'd learned that changing the rules or flipping expectations around was the best way to get a different reaction. It at the very least changed the tone of the conversation.

"Truth is the truth. I don't feel sorry for myself. My grandparents were great and supportive. Not everyone can have what you have, Lurlene. I'm sorry if people pressured you to include me in stuff when we were kids. We weren't friends and you shouldn't have to invite people you don't want around because others say so. Or because you're supposed to feel sorry for them. Especially at thirteen. Inviting every girl in your class is silly crap from first grade. But in small towns, people talk. I'm sure your mama just wanted you to look like the bigger person who was being nice." I smiled.

"Right. I'm not."

"You shouldn't have to be. Teenagers are supposed to be selfish."

"Exactly." Lurlene finished her drink. "Another, please."

Katie looked at me. I nodded, and she poured but went lighter on the liquor.

"As an adult, you decide what's right and wrong for you. It's freer than being bullied by other kids or your parents. I'm sure you'd have helped Luke with Jeff and Pete, taken them all in and cooked for them, helped with their laundry and all of it. Hospitality and open doors for all, right?" I asked.

"Sure. I'm a great cook." Lurlene grabbed a pretzel from the bar bowl and nibbled.

"Even with beauty school and helping at your dad's store, you'd still be there for all your guests and never work on a Sunday. Plus you'd do all the pastor's wife's traditional work and fill in wherever needed. Heck, Luke didn't like me working here to help Katie, so you'd stop drinking here and be at home with him — sewing or praying," I teased.

She shot me a side eye. "When you've found the right person, drinking at home is cheaper. I come here to be sociable."

"Right, that's why you were crappy to Martha and me. How is it possible we're worthy of any of your time? You're not getting any younger. That clock is ticking. I think I can hear it." I leaned in.

Katie stifled a laugh.

"You're a bitch," Lurlene said.

Gus walked up. "What's going on?"

"Your girlfriend is a bitch. She's being all mean saying I'm old." Lurlene hopped to her feet and lost a heel.

"I didn't say that. I simply suggested she go talk to the single men since she's here for socializing and she already sent Martha off nearly in tears," I replied.

"Okay, that's enough. Miss Lurlene, we're giving you a ride home," Gus informed her.

"No, I'm not done." She put her hands on her hips. "It's perfectly legal to drink in a bar."

"But you came in drunk. You had some already. It's time to go. Or I'll write you a ticket for public intoxication."

"I'm in a bar. I didn't drive. I can get as drunk as I want." She stomped her one heel.

"No, you can't." Katie pointed at the sign that read, *We reserve the right to deny service to anyone.* "You're cut off. Take the free ride home."

"It's all her fault. You're my curse, Belle." Lurlene glared at me.

I finished my drink, hopped off the barstool and picked up her one shoe that had slid away. "I'm ready when you are."

"Sorry the night got cut so short," he said.

I shrugged. "In your job, emergencies will happen. But if you ever put her over me when it's not a real emergency, we'll have a problem. This is just dropping her off on the way home. I can't wait to see what her mom has to say about that."

"Don't. I'll sneak in the back," she insisted.

Gus and I smiled. "Honey, you couldn't sneak into a pumpkin patch without stepping on five pumpkins and a hound dog's tail," Gus teased.

Gus put her in the back of his SUV.

"You're just loving me back here," Lurlene grumbled.

I sat in the passenger seat. "I'm not hating it, but mainly it's so you don't puke on us."

Gus sighed. "It's easier to clean out that back seat if you do puke. It's all hard plastic back there."

"I don't puke. It's a waste of alcohol." Lurlene batted at the protective plastic that divided the front and back seat. "This makes me look like a criminal."

"You'll be home soon," Gus promised.

She smiled. "And where are you taking Miss Belle? Home to granny or out for a long drive for a little fun? Trust me, Belle, when he's had his fun, he'll be over you. Wild girl, just like her momma."

"I'd say that's not fair, but you are a drunk like yours," I teased.

She slammed her hand into the plastic divider and called me a few choice names.

Gus closed the section so we couldn't hear her comments.

"Another suspect?" I asked.

He nodded. "She wanted Luke. I don't think she'd kill for him, but I'm worried she'll go after you one of these years."

I laughed. "She just wants to win. She'd never hurt Luke because he was the prize, in her mind."

"But if he chose you and not her, she might try to scare him," Gus concluded.

"Lurlene's dad owns the feed and supply store. I doubt she'd touch a snake directly, but there are plenty of men working there who probably handle snakes. Do a favor for the boss' pretty daughter? They probably thought it was a prank." I waved off the notion.

"I'll add it to the list, but I'm not sure a snake in the house would send the message Lurlene was going for," Gus replied.

Chapter Eight

The funeral was the most awkward I'd ever attended. Playing the piano for the choir was the normal part. Megan breaking down a couple of songs in was odd. I'd told her to opt out of singing, but she'd insisted on the tribute.

A big part of it was a strange pastor no one knew in our church, except Pete. People did the readings and the preacher talked about Luke's devotion to his flock.

I focused on the music and the people. There were two new faces in the crowd — beyond Luke's parents, a few close friends who were seated with Pete. Jeff sat in the back, which felt wrong somehow. He'd known Luke better than most of us.

"That concludes our service. As many of you know, Luke's brother and parents will take his remains home and have them buried in the family plot. You're all welcome to join the family for refreshments in the entrance area of the church. We all pray that the person behind Luke's untimely death be brought to justice on Earth and in Heaven."

I played some exit music and once the church was empty, I dashed out to help Gran. There was sweet tea, lemonade and coffee as well as a ton of different things to nibble on. Our apple pie slices and cobbler squares were popular.

Gran was standing behind the tables, helping direct people. "I'll get you a chair," I offered.

Gus beat me to it and set a chair behind Gran like he'd read my mind. The guy had a lot of good points. *Maybe I was too hasty and overreacted about the ex?*

I smiled at him. "Thank you."

He winked. "Get back there and help. Keep an eye on things. I saw two people I need to talk to."

Martha walked up. "I can help," she offered.

Martha's daughters ran up to show Gran the cards they'd made for the pastor.

"You're sure? You've got a handful," I said.

"Go on, I've got this. Gran loves the girls, the girls love her and her treats and it's less depressing for them back here. You go work with Gus." Martha winked.

"I'm not sure I'm much help." I shrugged it off.

"Go." Gran sipped her sweet tea and helped the girls to plastic cups of lemonade.

"I'll be back to check." I grabbed a couple of sweet teas and headed for the sheriff.

Harry, Katie's brother, walked up to me. "You okay?" he asked.

"Yeah, it's weird, but we'll get through it. Martha is with Gran, helping."

"I'll keep an eye on her. Lurlene is in rare form. I heard how she was to you at the bar. She shouldn't take her pain out on other people."

"I don't think Lurlene knows any other way. Thanks for keeping an eye on them. You could just ask her out," I teased.

"Your gran? Way too old for me," he joked.

"Men." I sighed.

Katie smiled at me, and I headed over. "How's it going?"

She adjusted her bangle bracelets. "Harry is going after Martha, I assume."

"You don't approve?" I inquired.

Katie shook her head. "No, Martha's great. She could use a little more confidence, but not everyone has a big dream. The kids are nice and cute."

"Anything else interesting around here today?" I asked softly.

"Two people no one recognized. Gus is trying to talk to them. Or is that tea for me?" Katie joked.

I rolled my eyes. "I'm just trying to be useful. It's a funeral."

I moved on to find Gus talking to a woman. She was pretty and young, but her eyes were red.

"Sheriff." I offered him a glass.

"Miss Baxter, this is Miss Henley. She played piano for Luke at a prior church. Apparently, that didn't work out," Gus said.

"I'm sorry. So nice of you to come out today," I replied.

She sniffed into a tissue. "I needed to see that he was really gone, but I didn't expect cremation."

"We didn't either. But his family wanted it," Gus confirmed.

"He had a habit of dating members from the choir. It didn't always work out. He fired me from the choir when we didn't work out," Ms. Henley said.

"We didn't work out either. I guess he didn't have time to fire me. I wouldn't have been surprised, I suppose," I said.

"It wasn't just me. He dated others. It's crazy how he got away with so much. His death was fitting," she grumbled.

"Meaning?" I prompted.

"He was a snake. That's what took him out. I needed to know it was real. If you'll excuse me, I have a couple hours' drive home."

"A couple hours?" I asked.

She nodded. "I moved away from that church and town. I needed a fresh start."

"I hope you got what you needed here," I added.

"Closure is complicated, but he won't hurt me again." She smiled slightly.

"Was he in contact with at all you since he moved?" Gus asked.

"Not personally. I watched him on social media. He'd send updates to our church's social media page — how he was doing. It was infuriating and emotional. Now it's done. Good luck finding a new pastor," she said.

"Is there anyone you can think of who wanted Luke dead? Who'd go to the trouble of putting a snake in his home?" Gus asked.

She shook her head. "Killing a pastor. That's a bold move and a big sin for a churchgoer. No, I can't imagine."

"Have a safe drive," I called.

"Not likely her," Gus concluded after she'd left.

I handed him the sweet tea. "I'd say no. She's right — avid churchgoers doing something like this? So

107

planned and deliberate. Who else were you wanting to talk to?"

"That guy, but he's dodging people. It's weird," Gus remarked.

"Let me try." I headed back to the table and got a piece of cobbler on a foam plate and a sweet tea in a plastic cup, making it seem like the guy could politely take it and dump it if he wanted to get away — no need to return cups or plates.

I walked right up to him like the welcome wagon on the porch of the church. "Refreshments?"

"No, I just wanted to pay my respects," he insisted.

"Well, the ashes are in the church. You're welcome to go through the crowd. Were you from his former parish, or family?" I asked casually.

"Not family. I'm sorry, I have to be going," he said.

"I don't mean to run you off. Take all the time you need," I offered.

He was gone.

Gus walked up. "Nice try."

"Sorry. Usually my chitchat works."

Gus took the cobbler. "You kept him around long enough for me to get a picture. One of the deputies got his license plate info. We'll look him up that way."

"Creepy." I sipped the tea.

Lurlene was there chatting with Angie Lowell.

"Did you get her alibi?" I asked.

"She was on a work trip. But we can't prove she didn't swing by here on the way to or from her event. Nothing confirmed. She's making the right friends though. Lurlene is glaring daggers at you." He grinned.

"At us — she probably thinks we're dating. She thinks everyone feels sorry for me and not for her. That

that somehow got me the pastor and the sheriff. She's crazy," I said.

"The pastor was after you. Maybe he wanted to show me up?" Gus teased.

"Maybe he just knew I wanted to be the good girl and thought I'd play along and do all the pastor's wife work. Then he had a girl on the side," I complained.

"Figure out who yet?" he asked.

I tilted my head toward the core choir ladies. They were fussing over Megan, who couldn't stop crying. "She's always emotional, but this is extra."

Gus nodded. "Grab that bench over there. I'm going to hook her away."

I strolled to the bench and took a seat. Whatever he said seemed to charm the ladies and calm Megan. He steered her to get some lemonade and apple pie before heading over to me.

Megan locked eyes with me and her feet slowed, but she wouldn't be rude to the sheriff.

"How are you doing?" I asked.

She sat down and shrugged, proceeding to eat. "I can't believe you two are back together so fast. It looks tacky. Lurlene is having a field day."

I smiled. "I'm sure. We're not anything official. We're trying to solve the murder."

Megan looked at the sheriff. "I see. It sort of makes sense if she was using the pastor to make you jealous. But I think Belle is better than that."

"She is. We weren't officially anything. I had some trouble with an ex. Luke snuck in but I'm not holding any grudges. We'll find out who did this and justice will be served," he assured

"I'll be glad when it's all over." Megan sipped her drink.

Someone came over with a tray full of glasses of wine. Gus grabbed two and handed them to me and Megan. "Ladies."

"Thanks." I sipped the chilled white wine. If nothing else, it'd help relax me a tad.

Megan did the same thing then stood and turned around, spitting the wine into the bushes.

"Are you okay?" I asked.

"Fine. Sorry. I think I ate too much today. I'm going to go home. Please excuse me." She headed for the parking lot.

"Do you need help?" Gus offered.

"No, I'm fine. I'll be perfectly fine, thank you." She waved him away.

"Wine taste okay?" he asked me.

"Fine. Wonder what's bugging her. I had apple pie too. There's nothing wrong with the food." I took another sip of wine. "Oh."

"What?" Gus asked.

"I'm not sure. I don't want to start rumors," I said.

He sat next to me and leaned in. "It's not rumors if you're telling the police."

"Well, why would a woman not drink? I've seen her in the Buckle on a Friday night having a special. She doesn't drink a lot. What's so wrong with one glass of wine to toast the pastor?" I asked.

"She's in AA?" he guessed.

"That's one reason. But spitting it out like that? Very unladylike. If she didn't want it or doesn't drink, she'd just say so."

"What else is there to do?"

"She could've swallowed the sip and set it down. One toast and done or something. But not drinking a single drop..." I shook my head. "Spitting it out? That's someone who is on meds that make drinking dangerous...or she's pregnant."

Gus' eyebrow arched. "That's interesting."

Before we could debate more, Jeff walked up. "Sorry to interrupt. My compliments to the chef. Excellent cobbler and pie, Miss Baxter."

"Thank you. Please take some extra with you for later. Did you know the man who was here? None of us recognized him," I said.

Jeff shook his head. "Sorry, I don't. Pete said I can move into the motel with him when I'm let out of the jail. I don't want to want trespass on anyone's hospitality."

"No worries. I'd like to hold on to you for a few more nights, just to make sure funeral visitors are gone. We'll have a talk about Angie and Ms. Henley, if you don't mind," Gus suggested.

Mr. Johnson didn't seem all at all flustered. "Sure. Ms. Henley was hurt. Angie was much more public about how she handled the breakup. People are different. Their relationships with Luke were different."

"Jeff, the Baxter shop is in need of a little electrical upgrade. Belle, Jeff shared that he did a lot of repairs and upgrades on his first churches. He might be able to help. I'm happy to help, but I'm not an electrician," Gus offered.

"Would you be interested in some work?" I asked.

Jeff perked up. "I'm happy to pay back some of the kindness. I actually was an apprentice electrician before I found my calling."

"Wonderful. Once you're free, come on over. Gus has tools and we have some as well." I smiled.

"Thank you. If I'm going to start my life over, that's not a bad place." He walked away with a bit of a spring in his step.

Chapter Nine

The next morning was slow at the shop because we'd contributed so many goodies for the funeral. Gran and her men were watching the store and planning what summer fests they might set up tables at. I made a bunch of muffins to keep myself occupied.

Gran padded in and grabbed a few fresh muffins. "You and Gus having fun?"

"We're trying to solve a murder," I replied.

"People are talking about you two. You spent most of the funeral together," she reminded me.

My shoulders slumped. "I'm sorry. I left you at the table with Martha. That wasn't fair to you or her. I wish I had a clone."

"Don't worry about me. I had my guys there too. People always come to chat when you have the good food. Martha and the girls were fun and Harry kept circling by to see if we needed anything. But you and Gus — if you don't want people to assume, you might want to dial back the time you're spending with him."

I shook my head. "You invited him to dinner. I thought you liked him."

"I do, but you know how people talk. Sometimes you don't realize how it looks. Especially with how recently you broke up with Luke," she pointed out.

"Gus and I are just working together right now. I was close to Luke, so it makes sense." I smiled weakly.

"I just don't want you to be upset again."

I hugged her. "I know. I want the murder solved right now. I'm going to take some muffins over to the station and check on everything."

Gran waved. "Have fun. No one is perfect."

"Every dog should have a few fleas. Wait, me or Gus?"

"Both." She shrugged.

"Jeff and Gus offered to help with the electrical. It's not at all flirty," I defended myself.

I bagged up a bunch of muffins and a couple of small jars of preserves then headed out. She joined her guys. "Have fun," Gran called.

"Bye," I called.

It was too far to walk but a short enough drive. Parking my old truck, I hoped I'd catch Gus here and not on a call or patrolling around.

I walked up and the deputies stood like I was the first lady of Tennessee or something.

"Hi. I brought muffins. Thought I could check on Jeff and talk with the sheriff," I informed.

Lou nodded. "I'll get the boss."

The guys opened the bags. Gus came out of the office and removed his hat. "Come on back, if you like." He grabbed a muffin.

I went into the office and he closed the door. This was exactly what Gran was talking about. But what could I do?

Chatting with all the deputies would've been tedious as they would all want to show off their theories. No doubt, Gus had already heard all of those already.

"Coffee?" he offered.

"No, thanks. I'm fine. Have you crossed any people off the suspect list?" I asked.

Gus sat behind the desk. "You, but plenty of people still think you're a suspect. Sorry, Mrs. Woodson has no motive and could've covered it up much longer, so she's clear. She was out to dinner with her niece when you and Luke were out at dinner, so that would've been the best option to put the snake in—when he was out."

"The church service would've been good too. Most people were in church. Someone could've planted the snake in the house. Under the bed or somewhere he wouldn't see immediately," I suggested.

"That'd be handy. We could rule out all the church attendees, but whoever did it had overnight and into Monday as well. Time of death clocked around nine in the morning, so the snake probably came out at night and wrapped around him to stay warm. When Luke tried to get free, the snake would've felt threatened and tightened around him."

"Is that what Animal Control said?" I asked.

"Yes, and I called up a few people who know snakes like this. With no pets in the house to eat, the snake might've viewed him as the only source of food but couldn't swallow him."

I shuddered. "Jeff couldn't have done it. Luke would've known if he had a snake with him. Why would he keep a snake if he'd lost everything else?"

"I agree, but it's curious timing. I'm waiting for a deep, dark secret," Gus said.

I frowned. "You seem to trust Jeff enough to let him walk around the funeral."

"With plenty of deputies and an ankle monitor," Gus added.

"Pete cares about his brother. I know they had issues, but I don't see him blowing into town and visiting to sneak a snake into his brother's house." I shook my head.

"I agree. Pete could've just stayed away. Unless there was a new development in their rift, but then why would Pete meet everyone and go to the trouble of attending a funeral? I mean there's Cain and Abel...could be symbolic, but they didn't use a snake."

I chuckled. "True. It's personal. The snake tempted Eve with the apple. Might be one of his exes who felt they were tempted."

"You putting yourself back on the list?" Gus asked.

I tried to stop the giggles, but something about the topic tickled me. "We barely kissed. The chemistry wasn't there. Not a temptation, sorry. The way Angie and Megan have all these feelings over him, it's very clear he was a rebound for me. But he was always seeing two women at once, it seems. So they were seriously pissed off, and you can't blame them. I wonder how many more ladies like them are out there. I had no clue, so it couldn't be part of my motive."

"I'm very glad," he said.

"Did you talk to Larry?"

Gus sighed. "Larry talked to Luke about his being gay. You said Luke's views were more conservative than you expected?"

"I'd never have gone out with him if I knew that. Working in Atlanta, I met so many people of all different religions, views and lifestyles. You don't always get that in a small town." I missed some things about the big city, but I'd never tell Gran.

"People like being with others who are similar," Gus explained.

"We're all the same. It's just little details."

"Gay is a detail."

"Sure. It only matters if you want to date that person. Otherwise, it doesn't change how you treat them...unless you want to set them up on a date, of course — then it affects your choice of person. Sorry, I'm rambling. Larry was looking for approval or something and Luke made him feel wrong and rejected. That would've pissed off his brothers, for sure. Plus Katie. But none of them would go the snake route," I replied.

"What do you think they'd do?" Gus asked.

"Katie would probably ban the pastor from her bar. He never came in much anyway, but if his only reason was to judge people or make them feel convicted of something, she wouldn't let him be there. The brothers might quit going to church and tell people why — if they did, Katie would too. But right now, Larry isn't totally out to everyone, I don't think, so that might be premature. Pastors come and go. They've lived here forever, so they wouldn't go drastic over some advice and disapproval. Now, if the pastor got into one of the brother's faces about it, saying Larry was going to hell and all that, they'd punch him, for a start. Those boys know how to use their fists, and family is family." I chewed my bottom lip.

There was a knock at the door. "You wanted to talk to Jeff?"

Gus waved him in. "Get a muffin or two?"

"Yes, thank you." Jeff nodded.

"We're going over the suspect list. Anyone else you'd think of from the old church?" Gus asked.

Jeff shook his head. "I wasn't a member, but I'm sure he upset a couple or two in counseling. He had a lot of opinions for never having been married."

"We're still looking at Angie and Megan, but I can't imagine those ladies handling a dangerous snake. Maybe that sounds sexist. I don't mean it to, but they're not ranching or farming families. They don't work in the vet office or deal with nature walks and such. I've looked into them. They're both church ladies who sew and work in retail." Gus shrugged.

"Luke wouldn't go after a woman who's tough and handles wild animals. He liked old-fashioned ladies. But those ladies tend to have men around them, fathers, brothers, brothers-in-law or nephews who'll step up. Luke picked women who didn't have that. No offense, Miss Baxter, but like you," Jeff informed.

"Katie's brothers would go after a guy who took advantage or hurt me," I said.

"Friends are good, but Luke still saw you as vulnerable—he would've seen himself as the man closest to you. If there are men around these women who were that hurt by Luke, they could be considered suspects. It might've been a warning or threat that got out of hand," Jeff suggested.

Gus made a few notes. "I'll look into that."

"What about Luke's parents? Any reason to believe anyone else in the family had any issues with Luke?" I asked Gus.

Jeff laughed. "No, his parents are good people. They'd never do anything to hurt their family."

"We're still talking to the local vet about getting a list of anyone who has brought a snake in as a pet. They had a staff changeover and their receptionist was still learning the system. I'll follow up on that and dig into the two women's lives," Gus replied.

"Why a python?" I wondered aloud.

"Meaning?" Gus asked.

"Rattlesnakes, cottonmouths and copperheads are all local. Easily captured in someone's backyard. Why go for a snake that's so much trouble or expense to get your hands on?" I asked.

"Handleability. Pythons can bite without sending you to the ER. If the snake is fed, it's not likely to try to bite or crush you. It'll try to get away. The others...some people handle them, but most hit 'em with a shovel first. Not if they're pets maybe, but wild snakes will defend themselves and bite. A pet-type python might play nice at first," Jeff suggested.

"You seem to know a lot about snakes," Gus said.

Jeff chuckled. "I collected frogs and stuff as a kid. A lot of reptiles, but my ma never let the dangerous snakes in the house."

"Well, I should let the sheriff get back to work." I stood. "Let me know if I can be of any help."

"I will." Gus held out his hand.

I shook it and tried to ignore the sparks.

"Good day. I'll be by to look at that electric as soon as they spring me," Jeff promised.

"Thanks so much." I showed myself out.

* * * *

My mind whirled on suspects all day, but nothing was clicking. The goal might not have been murder, which made it twice as hard to pin down who would do it. One group would willingly have scared the pastor. Another, much smaller, group would have loved to see him punished or taken out.

I was making up loaves of cinnamon bread dough to bake the next day while Gran put away leftovers and got her ice cream.

"You should watch some TV and relax. Tomorrow will be busier, but you're making dough for a week." She grabbed a spoon and her butter pecan.

"The people get one whiff of seriously crunchy cinnamon bread and it goes like hotcakes."

"True. We don't do it all the time." She sat in her recliner.

"Our sales could use a boost."

"What?" she called.

"Nothing," I replied.

"I think the sheriff is here," she advised.

"What?" I wiped my hands on the old apron with tiny spoons on the fabric. It always made me feel like Anne of Green Gables.

"Gus is here." Gran pointed.

"Great." I dashed into the kitchen and put the loaves in the fridge. After washing my hands quickly, I put away the milk, eggs and butter.

"Come in," Gran called.

I walked to the front room calmly. "Hello."

"Sorry to interrupt," Gus said.

"No, you're not," I reassured him.

"Apron," Gran whispered so only I could hear her and put the feet up in her chair.

"Right, sorry." I untied the apron and lifted it from my neck. I went back to the kitchen and hung it in the mud room.

I came back to the living room.

"I didn't mean to interrupt the work. I just wanted to inform you that I'm going to talk to Dillon and the rest of the guys in the RV. Since it's on your property, I didn't want you to get spooked."

"What for?" Gran asked.

"I got the list from the local vets today. Who has pet snakes was our focus. Now they haven't been around much, but when I was in Animal Control checking on the murderous snake, someone there said he believed he'd heard the band guys talking about having a snake cage in their RV. One of them said they'd owned a snake at one point. I don't think it's now, but I have to ask," Gus explained.

"You're friends with them. They'd have told you if they had a snake," I said.

Gus smirked. "I play with them a little, but I don't go on the road, and I'm not living in an RV. That's a hobby—it's not my job. I have to follow every lead."

"Of course. I'm sure the boys won't mind. Did you see how they cleaned up the yard and repaired the fence? Now Duke has a dog run and we have a couple pens for animals whenever we get around to that," Gran remarked.

"I haven't seen, but I'll be sure to admire it tonight. Can we go out through the back and turn on whatever lights?" Gus asked.

"Sure." I led the way and flipped on the back lights. The RV lights were on too.

I walked with him. "Nice stretch of the legs. But then they don't bother us if they're practicing or playing music."

"Far from the neighbors too. They're considerate for a band," he teased.

Gus shone his flashlight on the pens and beyond.

"Heard on your offer yet?" I asked.

"Not yet. Thing go slow in the south."

"Nothing like going from a big city to a small town to remind you of that." I walked up the steps and knocked on the RV.

Dillon answered. "Lovely Belle and the sheriff. Come in."

"Drinking?" Gus asked.

"Just a little. Our night off, so we relax. Sit."

"Belle, not sure if you've been introduced to everyone properly. These guys tend to stick to the stage. That's Grant, Vic, Jackson and Troll. Beer?" Dillon offered.

"No, thanks."

There was no place that looked clean enough to sit on—shag carpet in burnt orange and a green plaid couch that looked like it was going to give out. There was a kitchen table where the guys looked to be playing cards.

"Nothing for me. I just wanted to ask you guys something. I heard you had a snake at one point. I just need to make sure it wasn't recently and wasn't a python," he said.

"Oh no, Troll used to have a rat snake," Dillon mentioned.

Troll had a lot of facial hair and long curly hair I'd kill for. He just needed to comb it more. "I got the RV from my uncle. He was a hoarder, so it was full of junk, just like his house. Both had a mice problem. We cleaned it out and set traps, but I got a rat snake to keep it clean. Some of those nightmares, I can still hear the squeaking and snapping."

"It's okay, man. Been clean for years." Dillon clapped his friend on the back. "Someone broke into the RV one night and tipped over the enclosure. Snake got out. We had no more mice, so we didn't get another snake. I felt bad buying mice to feed it."

Gus nodded. "Makes sense. Any reason you guys have a problem with the pastor?"

The guys shook their heads negatively. "Unless he was bad to Mrs. B or Belle," Dillon replied.

"We're not big on church going," Troll added.

I looked up a rat snake on my phone. "Oh, those snakes look nothing like each other."

"Nope. But we're happy to let you search if you want. Not much space to hide crap," Dillon offered.

"No, that's all I need." Gus shook their hands. "Have a good night."

"Night," I said.

I headed for the door and made it down the rickety stairs. Headlights in the driveway caught my eye.

"Who is it now?" I asked.

Gus followed me. The truck pulled all the way back, and passed the house near the garage. There was a pullout for farming deliveries.

"Can I help you?" I asked.

"Belle Baxter?" a hulky and potbellied truck driver asked.

"That's me." I stepped closer and the sound and smell of livestock hit me.

"It's all pre-paid. Sign here," he instructed.

I signed. "What is it?"

"Six standard goats and six pygmy goats. Suitable for breeding, disease free and so on. Here you go." He handed me papers. "Where do you want them?"

"There are two pens over there. Do you have any feed? This is sort of a surprise."

"Yeah. It'll be unloaded with them. You can water them?" he asked.

"There are troughs in there. I'll get a bucket." I walked to the house and found an old bucket in the mudroom. I filled it from the hose outside and carried it back.

"Who sent these?" I asked, not looking at Gus.

"It's all the paperwork." The truck driver released the big goats in the bigger pen.

I looked at the papers. "Luke."

Gus filled the trough in one pen. "I'll get more."

"Thanks." I stared at the papers in disbelief.

"They're for breeding, so you only got a couple of boys in there. Know what you're doing?"

"Sort of, thanks." I smiled.

Gus filled the other water trough. "Did you know he was going to do this?"

I laughed. "Does it look like I knew? Why would he do this?"

"Not all bad," Gus suggested.

"He must've ordered these before I dumped him." I felt awful.

"And died before he could cancel them," Gus added.

"I'm going to unload them." The truck driver stuck feed in both pens and headed back to his rig.

"Thanks," I called.

The band members checked out the goats and made sure the pen was sturdy enough.

"I was going to wait until I had a barn put up. Even one of those modular ones to keep them warm and out of the weather," I explained.

Gus sighed. "He jumped the gun."

"But they're so expensive. I can't believe he did this." I walked up and petted one of the pygmy goats.

Gran opened the back door. "Who was that?"

"We've got goats, Gran," I announced.

She carefully walked out to the pen. "Little ones and big ones. Cute."

"Luke sent them." I leaned on the pen. "What do we do?"

Gran looked up. "Thanks. Now we need men to build a barn. I'll send the guys to the feed supply store tomorrow for goat feed."

"This is crazy," I said.

"I'll start knitting little pajamas for the little ones. Keep them warm," Gran replied.

"How much? I gotta have a little goat in PJs," Troll insisted.

"What?" Gus asked.

"People have them as pets and dress them up." Dillon chuckled.

I felt a bit overwhelmed. "Gran, you don't have to knit anything. We can get baby clothes at the thrift shop."

"Used clothes? Not for our babies." She petted the little ones then headed back to the house.

Chapter Ten

A couple of weeks later, Martha and I were headed to our bartending course for the state license. I sent up a quick prayer that my old white truck would hang in there.

"How are things with Harry?" I teased Martha as I drove us to the commuter college on the outskirts of Nashville.

Martha giggled. "He's sweet. I'm not sure if he's serious. Most men don't want to take on kids."

I rolled my eyes. "Harry isn't a bad guy. He grew up in a house where the dads didn't hang around or even visit. He wouldn't be like that."

"He's taking things slow," she added.

I nodded. "Good. No rush. Your ex being a jerk?"

She sighed. "He's not thrilled. Harry and I aren't even anything official yet, but men get territorial. I get it, he wants to know who is around the kids, but Harry is a good guy."

"Darn right he's a good guy. Katie's brothers stood up for me when no other kids ever would," I assured her.

"He is. I know he's a great guy. The whole drama with Luke made me a little nervous, but clearly Luke was just more conservative."

I bit my lower lip and tried to ignore the oil light that was on my dashboard. "Did Harry tell you exactly what went down with Luke?"

Martha fidgeted with her hair. "Larry wanted to talk to Luke. Harry found out about it because Larry was upset. That's sort of how Larry's sexuality came out. I think Katie knew, and a bunch of people who work at the bar. Larry got upset. I think Luke might've said something to someone or threatened to out him."

"That's awful. No wonder there was all that tension," I pondered.

"Yeah, but neither Harry nor Larry would hurt anyone. I don't know David as well, but I can't imagine."

"He's been around less," I agreed. "But he's harmless. Hard-working like the rest of them."

"Harry said he was training for a new job. Long-haul truck driving. I guess it's good money." Martha shrugged.

It made me think about Ed and how Luke had supposedly helped the wife and kid to get away, but I hadn't seen Ed at the bar.

"You okay?" Martha asked.

"Sure." I pulled into the right lane.

"You drove past the car place you said you wanted to get an oil change," she reminded me.

"Right. I'm so frazzled." I turned right, and luckily there was an access road on the side of the expressway.

I got to the car place and they promised it'd be done in an hour with all the free checks.

"Just change the oil," I replied.

We walked next door to the community college classrooms. It felt like something between high school, with all the bulletin boards and meeting signs, and a community center. The worn tiled floor and scuffed paint on the walls showed this was no fancy high-priced college. I found the room and it had theater seating and was pretty full already.

"There is a garage in town," Martha commented.

We sat down and settled in. "I know, but then they want to fix everything. They see my old truck and think it'll be a goldmine. I feel terrible because I can't afford to fix half of the things it could use. I can barely afford what it needs. They need business, but it's cheaper here."

"I get it. If my parents weren't helping, I'd be screwed. My ex only pays support because my dad threatened to come to his work with a baseball bat and call him out for being a deadbeat dad in front of his boss. Some men, it's like they can't just do the right thing—if it makes them look weak, they have to fight. He can't give in to me, but my dad, well, that's different."

"Why?" I asked.

"Some weird knuckle-dragging genetic thing in their boxers region." She blushed.

I laughed.

A guy walked up to the front and the chatter settled down. He began with a boring intro about who he was and how long he'd been bartending at the trendiest places in Nashville.

Then more boring parts. *Go around the room and say why you're here.* Weren't we all here for the same reason?

Then the second guy turned so he could see everyone. He was in one of the front rows. He was also the guy who'd been lingering around Luke's funeral, the guy who no one had known. Rubbing my eyes, I wondered if I was imagining things. I tried to get a better angle and wished I had binoculars. He'd left the funeral before anyone had chatted with him enough. He also hadn't signed the guest book or left a card. Pete had let me snoop a bit through things after the funeral.

"Hi. I'm Ray and I'm hoping to open my own bar in the future. This seemed like a good place to start. Get certified and work at a few in my off hours," he answered.

"Dream big. I like it," the teacher responded.

When they made it to me and Martha, we both had the same answer.

"My best friend owns the big bar in a small town and I help behind the bar sometimes. I've worked as a barista, so it's a lot of crossover skills, but I want to be legit," I explained.

Martha added that she'd love to create new cocktails, but that was that and we settled in for legal stuff — what we could do, couldn't do and had to do to keep our certification. We got a little book of rules and a notepad to take notes.

I'd gone to college for hospitality and this felt like I was in high school detention. Normally I was positive, but I was going backward, not forward. Then again, if I'd done a community-type college, I wouldn't have student loans to pay off. But my proper college experience was full of good memories and opportunities small-town life just didn't have.

With my qualifications and experience, I could run a five-star hotel. I had never tended bar, so I'd never had this certificate. As he droned on, I realized I knew everything he was saying from working in a big hotel. Our bar had the same rules — even if I'd bartended there, I had to know those rules and enforce them in guests or patrons.

My brain kept wandering to Ray.

* * * *

When class ended, I walked down to the front and boldly introduced myself. Gran would never have approved. *Young ladies don't go chasing after men. Men do the chasing and a lady makes sure he's of good quality before she lets herself get caught...*

"Sorry, I don't mean to intrude, but I think I saw you at the funeral the other day. For Pastor Luke?" I asked.

"I stopped by to pay my respects. I didn't know many people there, so I didn't stay long, I didn't want to overstep. I'm sorry — you are?" Ray asked.

"Belle Baxter. Luke and I dated for a bit and I'm always curious to meet friends of his. Were you a member of his church, or maybe a friend from college?"

Ray looked uncomfortable. "Did you follow me here?"

"No, it's a coincidence. My friend and I really are helping a friend who owns a bar. We need this certification, but I never imagined I'd find you here. I feel like I didn't really know Luke. I guess it always felt like there was a distance." I frowned.

"Yeah, he kept himself to himself. He had a men's group where he talked about more traditional stuff. How men still feel defined by their work and responsible for their families. Women working doesn't change those old-fashioned ideas. Men judge each other," Ray explained.

"Were you part of that group?"

Ray nodded. "I was going through a divorce. You were dating him? Pretty and kind, seems right."

"Yeah, but apparently there's someone else. That's a pattern of his?" I asked.

"In the bible, men had more than one wife. He had some out-there theories." Ray rubbed the back of his neck.

"That's insane," I remarked.

Ray smiled. "Luke always tried to show one face to the public. He had another set of teachings for people who wanted to give up control and just believe—just follow no matter what. Like life would be simpler."

"Definitely not me."

"Then it wouldn't have worked out with you two. I'm sorry for your loss, but he has a lot of enemies out there. If you're trying to solve it, it could take years," Ray warned.

"You think it was murder? A snake might just have been to scare him."

Martha walked down. "Sorry, I was chatting. Hi, I'm Martha."

Ray shook her hand. "Hi."

"Ray was telling me Luke has a lot of enemies out there," I informed.

"Oh, enemy enough to track him down in a new town and new church?" Martha asked.

"Depends. Some people let stuff go and others brood on it and can't move on," Ray explained.

"Maybe we could talk about suspects or who he hurt. I know he fired some people and some relationships got complicated. It might help us to sort out suspects. We could call the sheriff," I suggested.

"I actually have somewhere I have to be. I didn't expect to chitchat after class. I'll catch you next time and we can talk afterward." Ray walked off into the darkness of the parking lot.

"Have a good night," I called.

"Too much? Did I scare him off?" Martha asked.

"No more than I did." I bit my lower lip as we headed outside for our walk back to the car place.

"Next time, we'll bring Gus," Martha added.

"You should ask Harry out to dinner. Find out if Luke overreacted or got seriously upset when he was confronted—was he a danger?" The two of them had been hanging out and circling one another but not made an official date yet. Katie suspected Harry was worried about Martha's ex, unsure if Martha was ready for something real.

In my humble opinion, Martha needed something better and real.

Martha frowned. "That's kind of forward. Even if we're just trying to help the case."

"You're right. He wouldn't talk about the really scary stuff to you. He wouldn't want you to worry or feel unsafe," I replied.

Martha murmured in agreement. I heard texting noises.

I walked up the service desk. "Here for my car, name is Baxter," I informed them.

A guy stepped out from the back. "We did the oil change but noticed this in your back tire." He set a baggie containing a nail on the counter.

"A nail in my tire? Really? No one pointed it out when we pulled up." I folded my arms.

"We caught it before it made it into the tire. So we pulled it, plugged it and only charged you fifteen dollars." He smiled.

"Oldest trick in the book. Take off the charge," Martha insisted.

"Lady, we did you a favor. We could've left it," he scoffed.

"That would be negligence. Why don't I call the sheriff and let him sort it out?" I pulled out my cell phone.

"Fine, fine. No charge." He crossed it off the bill.

I paid him and got my keys. I checked my gas gauge, my mileage and the emergency twenty I kept shoved under my ashtray. I got inside and Martha piled in as well.

"Everything else okay?" she asked.

"Yeah, lesson learned. I trust the garage in town not to pull crap," I admitted.

* * * *

After dropping Martha off, I drove by the feed store. It was open until ten and it was ten minutes to.

"Miss Belle Baxter?" asked Lurlene's dad.

"Hi. Sorry I'm here so late. I need goat feed and to order some sort of modular barn." I smiled.

"How much goat feed?" he asked.

"Um, I have six regular-size goats and six pygmy-size goats. Can I get a month's worth?"

"It's not cheap," he warned.

"I didn't plan on getting the goats this soon, but they were a gift." I shrugged.

"I see." He flopped a book in front of me. "Modular barns."

"Late-night shopping?" asked a familiar voice.

I looked up and saw Gus. "Hi. Goat feed and modular enclosure. What do you think?"

He leaned over. "I'd get that for the big ones and that for the little ones."

"That looks like a doghouse," I said.

"It's about twice the size of Duke's doghouse," he agreed.

"Shouldn't I just get one big barn?"

He flipped the pages and pointed out the price.

"And dog houses look reasonable." I hoped the goats weren't a mistake.

"That's a goat shelter for at least ten full-size. We'll put up a better fence around the pen to keep the wind and weather out. Lots of hay inside and some blankets. We don't get that cold down here. Goats, cows and horses are tough animals — not house pets," he explained.

"Pygmy goats, this should fit a dozen and it's fully enclosed. Okay. Those two. Thanks."

"You're keeping them all then?" he asked.

"Yeah, I did want them. I can't see returning them. If I wait until everything is perfect, I'll never do it. I was saving up for it, so Luke did something nice for me. I don't fully understand him, but I can appreciate that he wasn't all bad."

Lurlene's dad handed me the ticket with the total cost. I initialed and pulled out my credit card.

"That includes delivery, right?" Gus asked.

"I've got a pickup. I can come get it," I said.

Lurlene's dad cleared his throat. "Free delivery and assembly when it's all arrived. You can take the feed now, if you want."

"Thanks, I will. Can we make the goat feed a monthly standing order?" I asked.

"I'll set it up to charge your card automatically," he offered.

"Fine. Lurlene isn't working tonight?"

"She's in class."

"Oh, fun. I'm sure she's top of her class in everything," I said.

He ripped off a receipt. "Sign here and then you can pull around back. They'll load the feed. Your enclosures will arrive in a week — we'll call when we have the exact date. Here's your receipt copies."

I took my bunch of papers. "Thanks. Have a good night."

"Good night."

Gus walked me to the door.

"Aren't you here for stuff?" I asked.

He shook his head. "I saw your truck. You had class too."

We exited the store and he opened my car door for me. "I did. Not at the beauty school. Over at the community extension, for bartending certification. I got my oil changed right nearby, but you need to hassle that place. They tried the nail-in-your-tire trick."

"Got it." He typed a note into his phone.

"Last time I don't trust local. Oh, and that mystery guy at the funeral is from one of Luke's old churches. He's in our class. He said there could be a lot of people who have stuff against Luke."

"I've been checking out Luke's old churches. I'm aware of some very upset people. He tried conversion counseling and group meetings for it. He's not qualified to do anything mental-health-related," Gus said.

"But so many pastors do." I climbed in the pickup and started it.

"Leave that side of things to me and the deputies. A lot of people to touch base with. Some parents are upset he spoke to their kids without their consent. One kid that we know of killed himself six months after Luke left their parish. We're looking into any connection with how Luke talked about subjects."

"He was gay?" I asked.

"That and his mom was a single mom, never married. So he was a bastard. Luke was a bit more judgmental and a bit less Jesus-loves-everyone than most pastors around here. But go get your feed. Let the employees close up. I'll follow you home and make sure you're safe. Then I'll swing by the shop tomorrow."

"Thanks, but I can make it home," I told him.

"Belle, I'm not being overly protective because you're a woman. I'm worried that you poking around the case might make you a target. You got free goats, were his girlfriend publicly, and now you're free and nosing around. Someone might think you're the killer and want revenge. I won't lose you," he insisted.

"You know what people will think of that."

"I don't care. Once we solve this case, I'm going to ask you out, and no more Luke or Dina nonsense. Our exes are in the past." He grinned.

"Fair enough." I kissed his cheek and rolled up the window.

I pulled around, got the feed and headed home. Honestly, I only glanced back a few times, eyes on the road. But I knew he was there looking out for me. The important part, he'd never told me to stop trying to get answers or investigate. Gus wasn't trying to change me or tell me how to be. True, he had more experience and authority, but my roots were deep in this small town. I wasn't going to let murders just happen...but this one might reach beyond our little world.

Chapter Eleven

With the morning rush over, I was blending up a new flavor of smoothie while Gran kept knitting those onesies for the pygmy goats.

"Gran, I promise I have an enclosure coming next week. We'll put hay and blankets in it. It'll be fine for a southern winter," I argued.

"But they'll look so cute," she countered.

I blended away with a mix of berries. The shade came out blue. I tasted it and liked it.

Pouring samples, I called Gran and her crew to the counter to try them.

The men liked it, but Gran wanted it a bit sweeter.

"You like strawberry. That's all you want in there," I teased Gran.

Just then the RV drove up and parked on the streets. The band guys piled out and entered the shop.

"What brings all of you here?" Gran asked.

"We lined up a few gigs in Kentucky. We'll be gone maybe a week or two weeks, if things go great. We stopped by for coffee, smoothies and snacks for the road."

"Sample this and I'll kick off the coffee," I said.

"That's really good." Dillon took another drink.

"Thanks." I brewed coffee and bagged up pastries. Once all the guys had sampled it and approved, I poured out smoothies for them.

The bell over the door rang again and Gus and Jeff walked in.

"We're here to look at the electrical box," Jeff explained.

"Sure thing. It's in the back on the far wall." I pointed in the general direction.

Gus and Jeff headed back. I checked on them as I grabbed some beverage carry trays.

"We can expand things, but it'll take a little rewiring and upgrading the fuses," he planned aloud.

"Now hold on," Gran said as she walked in. "What are you doing?"

"We need better electrical, Gran. The charging stations were a bit too much for the system."

"Well, I don't own the building. We have a lease. I'll call the owner and see if he wants to do the changes or pay for it," she suggested.

"Okay. Come on, guys, and try this. Free pastries for your efforts."

Gran was poking at her phone as I served up more smoothies. "Gran, want me to call?"

"I'll call. He's probably at work. I'll leave a message." She waved at me.

I never wanted to treat her like she was helpless, but people out there in the real world took advantage of the elderly sometimes.

"Why don't you have him call Gus and review what needs to be done? We don't get all that electrical stuff," I replied.

"Good idea." Gran brightened.

I turned and Gus was there. "Do you mind?"

"Not at all. I don't want anyone taking advantage of her either."

It was like he read my mind. "Thanks. Berry Blues Smoothie?"

He tried it. "Good. Blues?"

"It came out blue and my favorite songs from those guys are the bluesy ones." I smiled.

Jeff sipped his coffee. "Well, I'm available whenever. Anyone looking for a handyman can find me at the motel."

"Hey, it's not handyman work, but we could use someone to help us on the road. Drive, make sure no one steals our gear and that we stop drinking in time for shows," Dillon explained.

"Driver, roadie and chaperone?" Jeff laughed. "Why not?"

"What's it pay?" Gran asked.

"Food, place to crash and beer at the show," Dillon offered.

"He has room and board with Pete," I countered.

"Here I'm earning it. I'll go, but what about when I get back?" Jeff asked.

"I have some handyman stuff you can do around the house and help the boys when they go on tour. Plus here, if the landlord is fine with it. Maybe get your contractors' license or something," Gran suggested.

"Get your electrical certs in order," Gus agreed.

"That's a lot of guys in an RV," I teased.

Jeff waved it off. "I can pitch a tent in the summer. I'll find a place by winter."

"Oh, the goat enclosures. He can help put those up. We might need a real barn?" I suggested.

"Sounds like a welcoming little town." Jeff smiled. "I'm not very musical, but I can drive and help with stuff. But I don't drink anymore."

"Let's go," Dillon said.

The guys had coffees, smoothies and pastries for the road. The band plus Jeff piled into the RV. We waved them off as they headed out of town down Main Street.

Gus sipped his coffee. "Always something in small towns."

"Not bored of us yet?" I teased.

He looked like he wanted to kiss me, but there were way too many people in the room for that.

Martha walked up. "Hey, what's going on?"

Gran filled Martha in on the band development and Jeff going along.

"How are the goats?" Gus asked.

I smiled. "Being fed and watered daily. Making a mess. But a few people have already inquired about a baby goat or goat milk."

He smiled. "Glad you're adjusting."

"Do they bother you?" I asked.

Gus shook his head. "Gifts from exes happen. Dina's ring has been returned."

"Good call." I nodded.

"I've got to get to work. See you later." He grinned and headed out.

"He's sweet on you," Gran teased as soon as Gus was gone.

"We'll see. You watch the front. Martha and I have dishes in the back," I replied.

"Fun." Martha tied on her apron and followed me.

I cleaned out two blenders. "Sorry. I needed a break."

"I got you. Gran forgot to soak these bread pans, so they'll need extra muscle. What's with you and Gus?" Martha pulled out the dish soap and scrubber.

"Nothing new yet. You and Harry?" I teased.

She blushed. "We had lunch at work. Harry admitted he threatened Luke for what he said to Larry. Luke backed off and that was it. They have no snake connections. He said if he wanted to do something with a snake, he'd put a rattler in a hollowed-out bible or the lectern."

I laughed. "That's creative."

"But could they handle a rattlesnake well enough to do that? I don't think so. I'm pretty sure you can cross them off the suspect list. Now we should talk about the class. Did you do the reading?"

I shook my head. "It's all stuff I had to know for my degree, I just never took the certification. I'll look over it before tomorrow night."

"The girls really want to come over and see the goats. The mini ones," Martha said.

"Any time. They are cute." I smiled.

My phone beeped and Martha's did as well.

I checked my phone while her hands were still soapy. "Katie needs us both to work tonight."

"Sure thing." Martha gave me a thumbs up.

I texted Katie that tonight was good but just a reminder that we had class tomorrow night. Katie replied with a thumbs-up.

Martha wiped off her hands and replied.

"What's so big tonight? The band left town," Martha commented.

I shrugged. "No clue, but it's good practice for class. You can quiz me."

"Don't think I won't. You might like to sit at the back of the room, but we'll be at the top of the class," Martha teased.

"You can have good grades no matter where you sit. There's a trick to avoiding the mean girls, creepy guys and learning without the drama."

"High school wasn't much fun for you, was it?"

"Sure. You've just got to learn to make jokes first and ignore what others say. Sassy remarks just fly off the tongues of southern girls. Like...he's so dumb he sits on the TV and watches the sofa—bless his heart," I snarked.

Martha laughed.

I was happy to help a friend, but the license wasn't the SATs. It felt really wrong that I was looking forward to choir practice. Snooping about Pastor Luke and the murder was something I felt like I could make progress on. I just couldn't relax and enjoy small-town life with a murderer out there...

* * * *

The whispering stopped when I walked into the choir room.

I was used to that feeling. People loved to gossip. My grandparents had always been where my parents should've been, so some people would politely ask if my parents had died in a car crash or a fire... Others would eagerly fill them in on the truth.

Her daddy ran off before she was born so Maury couldn't tell him he was the father...

Her momma dropped that bun and left like she was deathly allergic to gluten.

She's the do-over baby, but what do you expect after how her momma turned out?

Bless her heart, that girl never had a chance…

Kids were mean and judgmental. Southern women were worse.

I was walking into the usual group of church ladies who'd been nice enough to me before, very nice to my face when I was dating the pastor and now looked at me like I had something to do with this.

"I don't know why we're even meeting. We don't have a new pastor yet. Or a guest one. The mayor is looking into hiring one," said one of the veteran members.

Mrs. Woodson nodded. "The mayor asked that we keep everything very status quo until we got a new pastor. Rehearse your normal stuff. Maybe you should elect a choir director for the interim?"

The women looked around.

"Luke always said a choir director caused stress. He preferred to work closely with us," Megan explained.

"It's just temporary so people don't feel like they're wasting their time. One person takes the lead for now. I could help, but I'm not musical," Mrs. Woodson admitted.

"Let Belle do it. She's just playing piano," someone suggested.

"Why her?" Megan asked.

A couple other women shared a look at Megan's overreaction.

"She isn't competing for solos or who sings what part. She knows music but just plays whatever," someone explained.

"It seems like a fair compromise. It should only take a few weeks or months to get a new pastor," Mrs. Woodson commented.

"No, not me. You don't want me," I insisted.

Megan glared at me. "Sweet and not at all competitive. No one believes your little act."

"Act?" I asked.

"Everyone knows you're trying to be Little Miss Perfect, but the truth is in the raising and the blood. Luke tried to help you, heal you and get you on the right track in life, but it didn't work. He wanted to look like a hero and you're the little darlin' who did nothing wrong but be born..."

"He was dating me for his image? Is that what you're trying to say?" I pressed.

"I can't believe Pastor Luke would." Mrs. Woodson began defending him.

Megan started to look a bit pale with a tinge of green.

"Are you okay?" I asked.

She waved us away. "Mrs. Woodson, so loyal and kind. You'd never say a mean word about anyone you worked for or with or even met in your life."

"No, I wouldn't. But I don't think that squabbling about things is any way to honor his memory," she scolded.

"I agree. Why don't we put this on hold and worry about it once we have a new pastor?" I suggested.

Mrs. Woodson nodded.

"Fine." Megan's word caught in her throat.

"But first you two girls should apologize and shake hands," Mrs. Woodson demanded.

We both looked at her like she was the mean schoolteacher.

Megan and I were roughly the same age. We weren't close to being friends, but this wasn't a respect-my-elders situation.

"I think walking away politely is fine," I suggested

"Your momma never taught you no manners," Megan taunted. "Oh sorry, your momma ran off and left you like the runt of the litter."

"Megan," Mrs. Woodson warned.

I walked up to her and held out my hand. Gran was always telling me to be the bigger person, but right now I felt like Godzilla and people were shooting missiles at me no matter what I did. "I'm sorry if I upset you, Megan. You seem unwell. I hope you feel better soon. Just remember that liars and gossips are conjoined twins."

She smacked my hand away and covered her mouth.

"She's going to be sick." I tried to step away to find the bucket they kept around for Sunday schoolers.

It was too late—she puked on my cowboy boots. Rage, disgust and the urge to vomit myself were all things I fought. I gently kicked the excess off my boots.

"Are you okay?" Mrs. Woodson asked Megan.

"I'm fine. I'm so sorry. I must've eaten something that didn't agree with me," Megan lied.

"Please, you've been looking nauseated since before the funeral. You should see a doctor, because the flu doesn't last a month, Megan. If you're sick, please stay home so as not to spread it around. If it's something else, I've heard dry toast or crackers help." I turned and stormed out of the church.

I threw my gross boots in the back of my truck and drove home barefoot.

I'd never been so grateful that I picked my boots this morning. None of that evil woman's puke got on my skin. I'd just have to hose down the boots and my truck bed at home, then re-protect my leather.

What is wrong with that woman? She always looked like she was feeling ill. I'd thought it might be for sympathy before, because she'd lost Luke. Clearly it was something deeper. If the woman hadn't had the brains to take a pregnancy test, she should. With those symptoms, she wouldn't fool people for long.

Chapter Twelve

The puke incident was the talk of the town. I was getting smiles and nods at the Buckle. It was kind of embarrassing, someone throwing up on my shoes. But I'd stood up for myself and I wasn't the one getting sick.

Martha laughed after hearing the full story, despite her being one of the nicest people I knew. "You're mean, Belle Baxter."

"Mean? I had to take two showers after I rinsed, scrubbed and polished my boots perfect again. These weren't 'mucking the goat pen' rubber boots — these were my only pair of cowboy boots. Seriously, don't go out in public if you're ill or can't control yourself in the morning. It's just gross. She should be ashamed. That girl has her nose stuck up so high in the air she'd drown in a rainstorm. I never said she was pregnant. I don't know for sure."

"That's the rumor around town," Katie explained.

"Rumor? No one knows. She should've seen a doctor," I argued.

Katie held up a hand. "It's not our business. And if it's Luke's, you are the very last person on the planet who should reach out to her."

"I didn't mean to suggest or expose. I can't believe she's trying to hide it for this long."

"I'm sure someone else in the choir who is a friend of hers is handling it. I'll make a few calls. You're not the only person in the world who can help," Katie claimed.

"I feel awful. I didn't know. I didn't even really suspect. I dismissed the idea—who wouldn't use protection?" I asked.

"Someone who wanted a baby. Maybe she thought she'd trap Luke into doing the right thing. A pastor playing games like that?" Katie shook her head as she typed on her phone.

"What's the draw tonight that's got this place so full? I know the band is off for a bit." I tried very lamely to change the subject.

"Line dancing. Gus promised to help lead. Can you help too?" Katie asked.

"No, I'm bartending. Dancing isn't work," I argued.

Martha walked up and put an order in. "Oh, Belle. The girls and I dropped by your house to see the goats after school. You were in choir practice, but Gran was so sweet. We got a few photos of the pygmy goats in the outfits. Look." She flipped through pictures on her phone.

"Those are really good, Martha," Katie agreed.

"Just with my phone," Martha grinned

"No, those are adorable. I could hang those in the shop," I said.

"What do goats in knit onesies have to do with preserves?" Katie asked.

I shrugged. "Nothing, but it's homey. They're great pictures. Especially the ones with the girls holding the goats. Personalize the place. Goats are another family business. Unless you don't want me to hang the ones with the girls."

"Are you kidding? They'll think they own the place," Martha warned. "They'd love it."

"The band should get you to take their promo photos. Men don't pay attention to lighting or angle unless it's boobs," Katie joked.

We all laughed.

"Men always think things are bigger than they are," Martha agreed.

More laughing from the women just as Gus walked up to the bar. Without his uniform, it felt a bit personal. I walked over. "What can I get you, Sheriff?"

"Look, I appreciate the help, but maybe a little less sleuthing?" Gus asked.

"What? I haven't been."

He cocked his head and rested his muscled arms on the bar. He was in a nicely fitting T-shirt and jeans. I couldn't not notice.

"You riled up some things at choir practice," he accused.

"No, Megan puked on my boots at choir practice. She's the talk of the town and I never spread rumors, even though I knew a while back she was knocked up. I should be the one pissed. My boyfriend at the time going behind my back. What sort of woman is Megan to behave like that?"

"You have the moral high ground — you want to slap her down? It's only making you look like you had something to do with Luke's death. Another motive," Gus replied.

My jaw dropped. "She trashed me. Ask Mrs. Woodson. You know, I'm sick of trying to be perfect and when I stand up for myself, people act like I'm the bad one. He was the cheater, but she knew about it. She let me be the fool. Now she wants pity?"

"She didn't want it announced," he explained.

"I didn't announce it. I suspected from her symptoms but that's not the same as seeing a test. I asked why she was still sick. I never slept with Luke — why would I assume she had?" I asked.

He smiled. "I get it, but when you're tough on someone, people take notice."

I shook my head. "I wasn't tough on her on purpose. But she deserved it. I don't know why people care what I think. I know they're really hard on me, like Megan was. If I can take it, so can she."

"I guess people think you're better than that," Gus replied.

I pulled out a shot glass and tapped it on the bar. "I try, but I take crap for my parents bailing on me. I step one toe away from being Miss Perfect and I'm the bad seed. Do you know how frustrating that is your entire life?"

He put his hand on mine to stop my tapping. "I'll have a shot and beer. You don't owe them anything, but if you're going to butt your nose in on investigations and try to solve murders—that's pushing into people's lives. You're not a cop and you have to go in with sympathy, even with suspects."

"I wasn't trying to talk to her about the case. It was just about a new pastor. But between us, I think she's your new main suspect." I poured the drinks.

"Would she really kill the father of her child?" he asked softly.

"Nice to see you rebounding. Belle doesn't stay single for long," Lurlene called from the other end of the bar.

I shot Gus a look.

He smirked. "Her you can be mean to. But you can also choose to dance with me."

"I don't like line dancing. Besides, my boots are trying to recover from today. I'm in gym shoes," I said.

Gus downed his shot. "I'd still rather dance with you than anyone else."

"Sweet." I looked around. If I let him go, plenty of other women would swarm. "But I'm working."

"I told you to go do it. That or sing. Gus is the feature, but he wanted you here," Katie insisted.

I looked at Gus. He shot Katie a glare.

"I wanted a date with you without the pressure or issues. We're helping Katie keep up patronage while the band is gone. Sing or dance?" he asked.

I frowned. "Dance. I don't need Gran to hear about me singing in public, ever."

"You've got a good voice," he replied.

I shook my head. "I'm not adding to the failure in my family. Everyone in and around Nashville wants to be a singer. There was a whole TV drama about it. When I get the urge to sing in public, I watch it, and see all the stress and time on the road — and those are people with labels behind them. I'm not setting myself up to fail with crazy dreams. I'm happy here, making smoothies, pastries or boilermakers."

"Fine, dancing." He took my hand.

"Finish your drink. I need one to do this." I pulled my hand away and did a shot.

Just then Angie walked in and sat down next to Gus.

"I heard. Congrats," she said.

I frowned. "I think you've got the wrong person to congratulate."

"Word is you got a dozen goats. Odd gift," Angie commented.

"Oh, the goats. Yeah, I have the goats. I was thinking about getting some on my own, so it wasn't something he came up with. They showed up after the funeral, and it was a total shock. Sweet, I guess."

"Generous."

"Luke was a cheater, apparently," I admitted.

Angie nodded. "He wanted a girlfriend that looked good on his arm. Secretly, he liked women a little bit older than him. Married, mature — not old, but there's a feeling about them."

"Megan," Gus concluded.

"She was divorced. Can you imagine if he was cheating on me with a married woman?" I asked.

"Some men think they can get away with anything," Angie said.

"Any idea why he likes more mature women?" Gus asked.

"Can I get a rum and Coke?" Angie asked.

"Sure." I grabbed a glass and made her drink.

She took a sip and looked around. "I'm not a gossip and I have no love lost for that man, but he never killed anyone. He played with his power and cheated on women, but murder is a bit much. His mother died when he was young. He only had his father and brothers growing up. He likes being taken care of, the center of attention. I hate to say a mommy type, but at least a housewife from the fifties."

"Belle would be a great mom," Gus replied.

Angie sighed. "I'm not saying she wouldn't. But she hasn't been married or had a kid yet. When everyone else expects you to take care of another person over and above yourself, it changes you."

"I take care of Gran, but she's still fairly independent, and she raised me." I pondered what Luke was thinking. "Why wouldn't he just date Megan since she was single?"

"To keep the power. He needed to be in charge." Angie sipped her drink.

"What if he got one of the women in his little game pregnant?" I wondered.

Angie grabbed her throat and coughed. "What?"

I poured her a glass of water and set it on the bar.

She sipped the water and cleared her throat. Her index finger extended toward me.

"No, no not me. We never got that far," I replied.

She took a deep breath. "He wanted kids, but who the mother would be—he was so picky. If things weren't working, he'd be rude and difficult until the woman ended it. He never wanted to be the bad guy. Insane, but he'd never acknowledge the kid."

"DNA sort of makes that stupid," Gus pointed out.

"Sure. I always assumed that's why he hopped around churches so much. It could be someone in his past or current. I'm sorry I'm not more help. Is someone really pregnant?" she asked.

Gus and I shared a look.

"Wow, if she told him and he rejected her—I wouldn't blame her." Angie folded her arms tight across her chest.

Lurlene scooted over. "Hey, Belle, don't make Gus puke too. We want to dance with him."

"I'm not what made Megan puke and you know it. You were so into Luke, wanting to be the pastor's wife—you're sure you didn't try to get him nailed down?" I asked her.

She glared and looked around. "No, he and I never dated. You're sure you and Megan don't have anything in common?"

"Sorry, I'm too much of a good girl. Now you'll call me a prude." I rolled my eyes.

"No, but bees go to the open flowers, not the dead ones," Lurlene pointed out.

"Watch it," Gus warned.

"And your dead ex got you goats. Is it creepy to keep them? Do you feel like they're watching you and will judge when you date other men? Oh, I'm sorry, Sheriff, are you two already a thing?"

"She's just jealous," I said.

"If I had a sob story about my childhood, I'd have men wanting to rescue me too," Lurlene taunted.

I looked at Gus and he slightly signaled *no* with his head. That was how it felt. When I told guys the truth, they liked to feel like they were making me feel special or safe.

"Jealousy is a bitch," Angie snapped. "Good night."

She dropped money on the bar. I closed her tab and took the rest as a tip.

"She just came by to cause trouble. Is she still a suspect?" Lurlene asked Gus.

He shrugged. "I haven't ruled her out. She came down here to follow up on gossip. She's invested and very interested."

"Nonsense charms the multitudes and plain sense is despised. Or maybe she came to help and to get some closure. Luke treated her badly too," I reminded.

"And nice Belle is back. So boring. Sell those dumb goats. No one wants them," Lurlene scoffed.

"Your dad is making money off the feed and I bought two enclosures. Why wouldn't people want them around?" I asked.

"Just smelly and dumb animals." Lurlene shuddered.

"You sound like a city girl," Gus teased.

Larry burst from the back room and looked spooked.

"You okay, Larry?" I asked.

"I found a snake in the storeroom. Injured rattler, nasty. I killed it." He poured himself a drink.

Gus got up. "I'll check it out."

Just then Katie got up on stage. "Come on, ladies and gents, cowgirls and boys, let's form some lines. Gus and Belle are your guides to learn how to tush push and strut around that dance floor. Beginners in the front, experts in the back and give yourself plenty of room. There will be lots of dancing, so if you feel crowded, wait for the next round."

"We have to do this first." I pouted and poured myself another shot.

"Fine. I'll check it after. Make sure no one goes back there and messes with anything. I'll get a deputy to meet you back there just in case." Gus sent a text quickly then reached for my hand.

I downed the shot and walked around the bar before taking his hand. Another snake. Was it a joke? A copycat? That was one too many to be a coincidence.

Instead of him standing up and leading the way to the floor, he leaned down and gave me a quick kiss on the lips. Nothing deep or intense, but it sent everyone in the room a message, especially me. We'd be all over town by morning.

Either the shot or Gus was making me warm and tingly, so I could temporarily forget about the third random snake. Lurlene was glaring at me like I'd stolen first prize in a pageant and she was runner-up. *Maybe letting Gus solve the murder without my help isn't such a bad idea?*

We hit the dance floor and I knew my gym shoes were a bad choice—I also knew that the suspects dancing in my head would never let me give up on trying to solve a mystery so close to home. This wasn't Atlanta—this was a small town I'd grown up in.

Chapter Thirteen

I stopped myself at two batches of scones. Without the band guys around, we didn't need to make as much food at the house. The shop was doing okay, but we didn't need to overstock. Part of me wanted to binge bake while trying to figure out the snakes.

None of the other snakes had resulted in death or any injury. All the snakes but the python were common for the area. Still, it was odd.

Duke's sharp bark split my ears — he was chasing the goats. I closed the window to dull the sound but watched as Gran tried to make them all friends. The goats were an added expense and more work, but they'd keep snakes away from the house and yard.

It'd be cute if I didn't have a headache. The pressure was changing in the air. Storms were coming and my sinuses felt it. A little nasal spray and aspirin was a start.

After starting the dishwasher, I went out through the back door and moved Duke to his run.

"He's getting better," Gran said.

"Duke wants to play with the goats. He's still a puppy. The goats have horns—they could really hurt him. We can't let them play when we're not here." I looked at the pygmy goats and they were just so cute.

"It's going to rain," she said.

I nodded. "The enclosures haven't arrived. We need something."

Gran smiled. "Milan and my boys are bringing their tall tent things. Not tents, but they block the sun and rain at tailgates or when they go fishing. A canopy. They can sit under the awning thing and drink beer and fish. It's not side protection, but it's a roof. We can put a tarp around it to help."

"Great. There are sides to the pen. It's not perfect— the pen will get muddy—but it'll dry," I said.

The guys drove up in a couple of trucks. I felt awful. *I should have a boyfriend to do this stuff.* They were my goats. I could set them up myself—I wasn't some damsel in distress. But southern men always wanted to help.

I walked up and tried to help carry, and they waved me off.

"Cover the big goats first. We can move the pygmies into their crate and put them in the mudroom. Let Duke have the rest of the house," I decided.

"Smart," Gran agreed.

Two of the guys rounded up the little goats and moved them inside. Gran and I made sure the pen for the big goats was fastened tight and I added an extra rope tie.

"If we can get the covers above that, they'll be good," I pointed out.

"We're on it." Milan carried one set of poles over.

I went to the faucet and filled another bucket of water. "Gran, why don't you go inside and get them a couple bowls of water and food."

"I'll put down some of Duke's puppy pads under the crate," she said.

"Why didn't I think of that?" I smiled.

I filled up the water and set the half-full bucket in the enclosure, just in case. I refilled their feed trough and made sure it was under the enclosure.

One canopy was in place and they were working on the second one when I felt the wind pick up.

Gran came out with the scones boxed. "It's getting late. We have to open."

"Ow," Milan yelped.

"What's wrong?" I asked.

He shook his head. The second canopy held and we scooted it into place. Gran walked up to Milan.

"I just pulled a muscle," Milan replied.

He had a hand on his chest.

"It still hurts?" I asked.

"An ache. It's a muscle." He waved it off.

I looked at the other guys and shook my head. "An ounce of prevention is worth a pound of cure. I'm calling nine-one-one."

"No, we'll go right to the ER. We'll get there faster than an ambulance coming out here," Gran insisted.

"I'll call Gus." I got behind the wheel as Gran got in next to me. I put the phone on speaker in the stand that stuck to my dashboard.

The guys took off ahead of me. I followed them, keeping up. They were a bit reckless, but luckily it was early and traffic was, well not much at all—it was a small town.

"Belle? What's wrong?" Gus answered the phone.

"Milan, I think he's having a heart attack. I said to call for an ambulance but they wanted to drive him there. So, there are three pickup trucks booking through town to the ER. Can we not get pulled over?" I asked.

"I'm coming." He hit the siren.

In a matter of minutes, Gus pulled in front of the guys and set the pace, leading us to the hospital in the next town.

Milan was taken in and I dropped Gran off at the door. I parked and dashed up to join Gran.

"They took him away. We just have to wait," Gran replied.

They group sat around, looking nervous.

Gus walked up. "Everyone okay?"

"We are, thanks. Milan is." I gestured to the back.

"You'll have to wait for info," Gus reassured.

Gran took my hand. "Belle, you have to go open the shop."

"You guys will be okay?" I asked.

"We'll be fine. We'll call you with updates," Gran promised.

"You got your phone?" I asked.

Gran opened her pocketbook and waved it for proof.

"Here are some singles for the vending machines. Get some coffee or tea." I slid the money into her purse.

"I have money," she fussed.

"Sometimes we don't always have singles. Just relax. Milan will be fine." I patted her shoulder

Gus smiled.

"Maybe I should stay?" I asked.

"No, you have to run our business," Gran insisted.

My heart was pounding. "See you guys later."

I walked out of the ER doors and sighed.

"I don't need any coffee," Gus teased.

I sighed. "That was an adrenaline jolt. He kept saying it was a pulled muscle. I hope that's all."

"At his age, honey, you did the right thing," Gus replied.

"*Honey*?" I shot him a look.

"You didn't punch me after the kiss, so I figured we were getting closer. Don't like honey?"

"Belle is good for now. Generalized endearments are too common," I snapped.

"Ah, I should ask you on a proper date first." He smirked. "What do you say?"

"Once we solve the murder, sure. But I have to get to work."

"You expect a police escort for free?" he asked.

I frowned. "No, for a real emergency. What did you think you were going to get?"

He folded his arms. "I was teasing."

"I know, but if you want a kiss, ask for it or kiss me. I'm not the type of girl to trade favors for other favors," I warned.

It sounded weird, but in Atlanta, people watched themselves a lot more. Men worried about sexual harassment accusations. It was nice to know people enough to recognize their intentions, but I wasn't going to let Gus play with blurred lines.

I got into my truck and headed for the shop. After opening up the shop, I put out the scones then fired up the coffee machines.

"Late start?" Martha asked as she walked in.

"Oh! Martha, you about scared me out of my heels. Yeah, Milan might be having a heart attack," I answered.

"You're not wearing heels, and what?" she asked.

"It's an expression. Milan came by to lend us a canopy for the goats since it's going to rain. What? You thought my grandmother had a sleepover guest?" I laughed.

"Why not?" Martha jumped to work. "I know it's a small town, but it's not the fifties."

"To Gran it is and always will be. What about you and Harry?" I teased.

She blushed. "Not while the girls are there."

"See." I set up the blender but didn't get ahead on that.

People started coming in for coffee and breakfast items. While the rush was busy, my mind was occupied with other things instead of Gus or Milan. I kept our customers happy and people stopped and asked about Gran and her guys.

Two hours later, I called Gran.

"Hi, dear, it's okay," Gran said.

"It wasn't a heart attack?"

"Oh, no, it was. Just a smallish one. They put in some stitches."

"Stents?" I asked.

"That's it. He's got to stay for a day or two, but he'll be fine. He's asking for scones."

"I think he'll live without them for a few days," I replied.

"Okay, well, we have to go. Doc is coming to check on him. Bye," she said.

Lurlene strolled in as Martha was hanging some of her pictures.

"Goats? Wow, your life just gets sadder and weirder," Lurlene scoffed.

"You just get meaner," Martha shot back.

"Just when I thought we were getting to be friends," I said.

Lurlene smirked. "Berry Smoothie, please."

I fired up the blender then added extra berries. I handed it over. "Here go you."

"You're just going to be nice. Too nice." Lurlene sighed and handed over her money.

I leaned on the wood counter. "I have had a rough morning, Lurlene. Gran is sitting in the hospital with Milan—he had a little heart attack. I need to be here then pick up Gran later."

"Then we have class," Martha reminded me.

"Dang it, class." I rubbed my eyes. "I don't have the energy to pick on you. You have work at your daddy's shop and beauty school, which is a cake walk for you. I've got Luke's murder hanging around and all these annoyed people."

"Gus is still buzzing around," Lurlene shot back.

"Did you not hear about Megan?" Martha asked Lurlene.

Lurlene rolled her eyes. "Of course, the town is as big as a pygmy goat's onesie. I guess Luke was a bad choice."

"All is not gold that glitters." I pulled out a fresh loaf of bread and began making sandwiches.

"I'll take a sandwich. Make up like five," she said.

"For your coworkers?" Martha moved behind the counter to help.

"No, I'll run them up to your Gran and friends." Lurlene stared me in the eye.

"You like being unpredictable, but you're nice deep down," I accused.

She sighed. "I assume I'm going to get a free box lunch out of the deal."

"Sure. But one more favor."

"What? You want my first born?" She admired her fancy nails.

I laughed. "Not for all the sweet tea in Tennessee. I'll give you some cash, make sure Gran has a bottle of water and an iced tea with her. Also make sure she hits the ladies' room. I don't want her getting dehydrated or getting turned around in the hospital when she needs to find a restroom. When she's out of her routine, I worry."

"Sure. Your gran is always sweet to me and everyone. You're lucky you still have her," Lurlene agreed.

"You like Gran, not me," I teased.

"I'll like you too for an extra cookie," she teased.

"A moment on the lips," Martha warned. "You've got such a perfect figure, Lurlene."

"I know. I'm just going to leave both of the cookies out at work. Make my momma nuts." Lurlene smiled.

"At least eat one. Don't get your mother after me either," I said.

Lurlene laughed. "Just get it all ready. I'll take it up there and get the old crew fed."

Martha and I worked in our usual assembly line. Lurlene left with the first six boxed lunches. Milan probably couldn't have his, but we'd thought of him and there was extra food if someone had skipped breakfast.

"Thanks, Lurlene," I called.

Katie walked in and her head snapped like church ladies when someone walked in late to service.

"What's going on? Backwards day? Aliens? It's the aliens?" Katie asked.

I smiled. "No, she's running lunch up to Gran and the guys at the hospital. Oddly nice of her, but I think she's relieved she dodged Luke, even though she acted like she wanted him."

"I heard about Milan. Do you need a hand?" Katie offered.

"Thanks. I'm just going to close after lunch, maybe two o'clock. Gran is at the hospital and I need to get her home, feed her and the animals, and then pick up Martha and go to class," I said.

"I can drive us if you want. Or drive myself," Martha offered.

"No, it's no trouble. I just don't want Gran driving when she's tired or shook up. I'm not sure I'll be able to drag her away," I explained.

"The guys have their pickups. They can drive her home. She can make herself dinner. She cooks for an army every day," Martha argued.

I glanced at Katie. "Fine. I'll have Harry run by there around five o'clock. If she's not home, he'll take her home. That way you're not counting on the over-eighty set. Those guys driving in the dark? Not the best idea."

"Thanks. I'll feel better," I said.

"Harry is so sweet." Martha smiled. "I'm sure he'd feed the goats and water them for you."

Katie rolled her eyes. "Yeah, he's a prince."

"That's asking a lot. I'll do it early," I replied.

"You said you wanted to study," Martha pointed out.

"Fine — Harry will take care of Gran and the goats. Get that class done. When are you solving that murder?"

"Gus, he's coming tonight because of Ray," I grumbled.

* * * *

Martha had prepared me well, but it was a good thing I knew most of this stuff from college. The quirks of Tennessee versus Georgia weren't that many. It was Gus in plainclothes sitting next to me that was a distraction. Not a good, flirty distraction—he was watching Ray. And Ray kept turning around, uneasily.

After class, Gus darted out and blocked Ray from trying to dodge him.

"Let's grab a drink," Gus suggested to Ray.

With Gus in full cop mode and not being at all subtle, Martha and I just went along for the ride. There was a chain restaurant in the strip mall down from the community college.

"Why so tense?" I asked.

"Let me handle this," Gus whispered in my ear.

We ordered drinks.

"Your friend here is trying to run me out of town," Ray accused.

"What town?" I asked.

"He's been snooping around Luke's house, Luke's church and watching your shop," Gus explained.

"You didn't tell me?" I turned on him so quickly I nearly smacked Martha with my ponytail.

"I didn't want you to change your habits. It wasn't just you—it was Megan as well," Gus told me.

I shot him a look that said we weren't done with this topic.

"Tell her the truth," Gus insisted.

"I'm a lawyer for Luke's parents. They had me handling his estate, as such. He did invest for his retirement, since his home was provided and so on. He wasn't poor *per se*." Ray frowned.

"So you weren't in this class by accident. And that's why you lingered but didn't talk much to people at the funeral," Martha concluded.

"Listening and watching people is usually good enough. Mrs. Woodson spoke to me, of course. I cleaned out the house for the family."

"His parents must be loaded if they have an attorney clean out a house and play errand boy," I figured.

"They didn't want Pete to do it and cover things up. They know their son had flaws and strong opinions. Pete might've hidden it or exploited it. He's a decent person, but not a pastor. Not what was expected of him," Ray explained.

"Pete said Luke was the chosen one and he was runner up. He didn't get the mentorship or help and went into another line of work." I filled in what I knew.

Ray nodded. "I'm sure he told you whatever he thought you'd believe. Did you check him out?"

I shook my head. "I wasn't interested in him that much. I broke up with Luke right before he was murdered, so I'm looped into this, but I did nothing."

"Pete did nothing to his brother either, but he's worried people will pin it on him. His parents want their son to rest in peace and their other son's name to be cleared. I've been trying to speak to Megan, but she doesn't trust me," Ray revealed.

"No kidding. She's learning, at least." I frowned.

"What do you want with Megan?" Gus asked.

My phone buzzed for a third time in my purse. I pulled it out. Gran was calling.

"Sorry, excuse me." I stepped outside. "Hello."

"Dear, Belle, where are you?" Gran asked.

"Gran, I'm at class. Are you okay?" I asked.

"Oh, yeah. Harry drove me home and I warmed up some leftovers. Lurlene was so sweet to bring us lunch. But I think I forgot to take my pills this morning. I took my afternoon ones," Gran said.

"Okay, Gran, you need to take your morning pills too. Drink a big glass of water and make sure to let Duke out," I reminded her.

"I know," she scolded.

"Okay, then just have dessert and watch TV. I'll be home in an hour max. Bye," I called.

"Wait, Milan is doing well. Where are your manners?" Gran asked.

"I'm sorry, Gran. I'm glad he's doing better, but I have to go to class. I'll tell you the rest when I get home. Bye." I hung up and slipped back into the room.

"Everything okay?" Martha asked.

"Gran's had a rough day." I sat down and took a deep breath.

"You two can go. I've got this," Gus said.

"Can I get a restraining order on him?" I asked Gus.

Ray held up his hand. "You approached me."

"After a class I thought we were both attending. You were stalking me here. You lied to me instead of just speaking to me at the funeral like a person. You could've said something about his will or whatever lawyers bring up," I suggested.

"You're not in his will. You're not carrying his child. The goats were ordered while he was still alive. His parents tried to cancel it," Ray replied.

"Classy." Martha rolled her eyes.

"I'd say I can return the goats, but my grandmother is getting attached to them."

"It's not the gift, but the appearance of things. You were his girlfriend at the time of ordering, no harm done. But they were worried Megan would be gifted with something more. We're not sure if Luke knew about the child," Ray explained.

Ray looked at Martha and me as though we'd have the answer.

"Sorry, we're not that close with Megan. Luke certainly wouldn't have given that away. This is crazier than a soap opera." I shook my head. "We'll be going. You sure you can't arrest him?"

"He'll get what he gets and a warning about staying away from you." Gus winked at me.

"We'll talk tomorrow," I added.

Martha and I piled into my pickup. "Men," she said.

"Don't I know it. Some random lawyer is trying to figure out if I'm pregnant. Gus lets me get stalked. Luke isn't getting any better." I headed home.

"Relax. Did you get any dinner?" Martha asked.

"No, I wasn't hungry. I read over the stuff for tonight, and after you left I cleaned the shop, prepped stuff for tomorrow and locked up. I made a list for the store. I need to get to the store tomorrow." I groaned.

"Do you need the stuff for the morning rush?" she asked.

I shook my head. "Nah, lunch was busy today. The second you want a time to be quiet so you can get ahead or deal with something else — it's nuts."

"Text me the list and I'll grab it before I come in. I'm off tomorrow, but I'll drop the girls off, hit the store and bring your stuff to the shop," she offered.

"I couldn't ask you to do that," I replied.

"I offered. Since Gran will be at the hospital, probably, I'll work if you want me to. I need to do my shopping anyway. I get a discount," she tempted.

"You're sure you don't mind shopping and working?" I asked.

"You're paying for the groceries. I'll put my stuff away and show up with yours, ready to work. I can use the money," Martha said.

"Right. Sounds great. thanks. I'll need help in the morning for sure. We'll see how it goes for the lunch," I answered.

"Done." She smiled as I pulled into her driveway. I fished fifty bucks from my purse. "Here. This should cover the list, but I'll reimburse you if it goes over. I'll text the list later. Thanks again!"

"No problem." She exited the car and waved.

Money was tight with all this help, but Gran wasn't getting younger. Business was good, but the juggle with goat expenses and what my car was going to need... I just had to have blind faith that it'd all work out. "Poverty is no disgrace but decidedly inconvenient."

I pulled into the drive and my headlights reflected on Harry chasing a goat.

Things were far from as okay as I'd expected.

Chapter Fourteen

I hopped out and helped Harry wrangle the big goats. "I thought you left and everything was fine? I called Gran," I said.

"It was, but she forgot to close the pen after giving them fresh water or something. She called when she saw them wandering around." He locked the pen. "Sorry, I should've made sure she did all her chores."

"No, thank you. It's not your fault. She should've waited for me. I fed and watered them before I left for class. She's all mixed up because of Milan. Her routine is off. I'm so sorry." I had to fix this. The whole reason I'd come home was to handle things just like this.

"Don't worry about it. It's a slow night at the bar. Without the band there, Katie is working hard to keep people coming. Jukebox music isn't a huge draw when Nashville is less than an hour away," Harry replied.

"And you and she are still being great friends to me. I'm just being a pain. I'll try to think of something to help, but I'm not much of a bar girl."

Harry shrugged. "It's not your thing. It's okay. You help bartending and never take any money. I stuck around while she heated up the leftovers and made sure the burners were all off, and the oven. She didn't like it, but she was tired."

"Thanks. You're a good friend." I hugged him. "You and Martha a thing?"

He pulled away and blushed. "I guess. I'm not trying to rush her. That ex of hers is a piece of work and I want to be sure she's ready for something serious."

"You don't want to be the rebound guy. I get it. Just don't be the jerk," I warned.

Gus pulled up and got out of his car.

"What brings you by?" I asked.

"Need a hand?" he asked.

I shook my head. "Harry helped. Thanks, you should go home. I don't want to ruin your whole night."

"Back to the Buckle, that's all. See ya." Harry waved. "Oh, Belle, if you're looking for something you can do to help Katie's bar? You and the sheriff could play and sing something. Even slow songs—people like dancing to them. Live music gets people out. Anyone can play any music they want on their phone, computer or tablet nowadays."

"Interesting suggestion. I like it. Bye." Gus smiled at Harry and looked at me.

"What? Gran called Katie—that's who she's supposed to call if she can't reach me. She should've called me but probably didn't want to admit she left the pen unlocked. I need to keep a closer eye on her. The bar is doing fine."

Gus hugged me. "You're amazing. Mrs. B needs to slow down. You need to find something you like, not just work all the time."

"When you own your own business, it's all work all the time. Gran doesn't want to be treated like a child. I get that." I glanced at the home and knew it was all on me. Gran needed a hand with most things.

"I run into plenty seniors who fall or have some sort of accident. Mrs. B thinks she's still forty and can handle whatever. She doesn't feel old, but one fall and she could break a hip. I heard about the fire in the kitchen. Stuff happens, but how fast we can react and handle it is based on our age and challenges. It's not treating her like a child," he said.

I nodded. "That's why she has other people to call. If you're serious about buying that land over there, you'd best think carefully. You'll be her first call all the time, after me."

Gus pulled me tight. "I think I can handle it. I'm guessing more homemade meals."

This was what I wanted. He was more like a partner, not a boss, and not a drag all the time. I went up on my tiptoes and kissed him.

Gran must've been watching from the window. Duke bounded outside and ran over to him.

"You don't herd goats so well," I teased the dog.

"Goats need a herding dog, and even then, they're stubborn. I'll get them some more water and leave you in peace."

"I got it. You don't have to," I said.

Gus smiled. "You need to let people help you."

"I do. Katie and Gus, Martha…" I replied.

"You resist my help." He looked good doing ranching chores.

I sighed. "I don't want a boss or a business partner in a boyfriend. Luke was a bad choice, but I didn't marry him or get too serious. We didn't even date that long."

"But you shut it all down with me," Gus accused.

"You need to make sure your past is past. No one wants to be a rebound," I explained.

He sighed. "You could never be that."

"We'll see. Let's find Luke's killer first. You can't keep me on the outside of things when I might be a target," I said.

"A target?" Gus chuckled.

"Hey, Angie got fired. Who knows what she and Luke used to be? Megan was sleeping with him while I was dating him. If his family knew about all this drama, I could find a snake under my bed to shut me up about Luke or scare me off," I pointed out.

"Okay then." Gus headed to the back door, Duke following happily.

"What are you doing?" I asked.

"Checking under your bed," he teased.

"No, what?" I followed him.

I turned off the outside lights and locked the door behind me out of habit.

"Sheriff, would you like something to drink?" Gran asked from her recliner.

She still had ice cream.

"Gran, it's after ten. I thought you'd be in bed," I said.

"The goats got out. We need a better lock on the pen." She shuffled to the kitchen and put the ice cream bowl and spoon in the sink.

"Okay, well, let me handle the goats from now on. I know the trick to locking it for now," I suggested.

"I'll look at it on my day off," Gus offered.

"It'd be so nice to have a man around the house who can fix things and help," Gran said.

"Jeff is coming back with the band, and he could use the work. Gus thinks he's safe, so you can put him to work."

"That is nice, since he needs it more. Gus can supervise. Maybe Jeff should be the new pastor?" Gran asked.

"One leap at a time, Gran." I filled Duke's dish and checked on the pygmy goats.

"Why are they in here?" Gus asked.

"It was supposed to rain today. I guess they were wrong. Hopefully those enclosures come in and we have a safe space for them." I smiled at the goats in colorful outfits.

"I'm going to check your room," Gus said.

"He's what?" Gran's face looked like she got skunked.

"I gave Gus heck for not telling me about this lawyer who was watching me for Luke's family. How do I know I'm not a target in this mess? Now he's checking for snakes, like I'm a crazy woman or I'm so literal," I mocked Gus.

Gus walked out. "No snakes, but I'm not treating you like you're crazy or being too anything. You had some good points. We didn't know all this stuff about Luke. Someone might not like him dating you when he was active socially elsewhere."

I smiled at how Gus chose his words carefully in front of Gran.

"He was knocking boots with Megan. I heard. Sad, that's what that woman is," Gran said.

"And Luke. He's cheating trash," I insisted.

"You can't say that about a pastor," Gran scolded.

I folded my arms. "A cheating pastor who knocked up one woman while he was dating someone else? He's trash."

"Speaking ill of the dead." Gran frowned. "I'm going to sleep."

"How's Milan?" I asked.

"Better. But they won't let him go home just yet. I'll go visit him tomorrow."

"Okay." I smiled at Gus as Gran headed to bed with Duke bounding after her.

Gus grinned. "She's got friends and support. That's good."

"They're all over seventy. They need some help. I'll drop her off," I said.

"I'll help, just let me know." He leaned down and kissed me.

I let the kiss linger for a moment then pulled back. "I can't let you help if you're going to lie or withhold information. She could've been in danger, or that lawyer could've followed her to get to me."

"You're right. I should've told you. But I identified him quickly. A lawyer from Nashville doesn't do the dirty work himself. If he sent a PI or some thug, that's different. He's just doing his job," Gus advised.

"Restraining order?" I pressed.

"I warned him, if he is seen in town again, I'll get a judge to sign TROs for you, your gran, Megan, Jeff and Mrs. Woodson. No lawyer wants that on his record."

"Okay, I need to get some sleep. Thanks for the help." I kissed his cheek.

"You are hard to get," he said as he went down the back steps.

I rolled my eyes. "I'm only planning on getting married once. No cheating, no drama and no walking away from commitments. Not everyone goes into things thinking like that, but my parents didn't think at all, it seems. About each other, Gran or me. I won't leave a mess for my family."

"Or end up like Megan." Gus turned and studied me.

A kernel of shame popped up in me. "It's not her fault Luke was murdered. You can't control that part of life. But she wasn't even his girlfriend. You know how people look at her around here, especially the older folks. She deserves what she gets for what she did. A young widow is one thing. I'd rather be a spinster than repeat my mother's mistakes. Night, Sheriff." I closed the door and tried to shrug off the judgmental attitude.

I didn't look down on others, Megan included. People made mistakes. I just wanted my mistakes to be my own and not a repeat of what my parents had done.

Locking up and turning out lights, I tidied up as I went. Once the dishwasher was loaded and the pygmy goats were settled, I went to bed.

Luke was a mystery to me. He'd been controlling and disapproving, yet he'd sent goats. An odd gift, that came with work and costs. Was it a test of what he'd been going to throw at me if we'd become more serious?

It was funny that anyone could suspect *me*—I didn't care enough about him to kill him. Breaking up with him was enough. Someone had been sending Luke a message, had been willing to kill him in the process. The snake had to have been planned and the person had to have had access to the residence. There was no sign of a break-in, so either Luke didn't lock his doors all the time or they had a key.

The mayor owned that church and the house Luke had lived in. The church board surely had keys. Mrs. Woodson, obviously. I yawned and crawled into bed, trying to figure out who else might be able to get in and out without force.

****

Gran cooked breakfast the next morning like nothing had happened. She looked much better too.

"Morning," I said.

"Breakfast is ready. We need to get to the shop and bake some cinnamon bread," she suggested.

"You don't want to spend the day at the hospital?" I asked.

"He'll be home in a day or two. It's fine. Maybe we'll swing by on the way home and pick up dinner from somewhere new?" she suggested.

"Sure, no class tonight. Only one more and that's done," I replied. "I'm going to feed and water the goats."

I opened the mudroom door and the little ones were restless.

"I know, guys." I slid the crate out and down the back steps, carried it to the pen and let the goats back into their home.

After lugging buckets of water and feed for both groups of goats, I realized why farm life was not for me in any serious way. Duke ran out beyond me, barking and sniffing the goats. The animals communicated and everyone went about their day, sniffing and hopping.

I went inside and had breakfast. Gran was in a mood and we were at the shop in no time. Everything was ready to open and we began on the cinnamon bread.

Six loaf pans were full and two were already in the oven.

"Sweet butter and honey jam." Gran set it out.

I washed my hands up to my elbows and wondered what smoothie would work today.

Martha showed up with the groceries and Gran fussed over her. They put stuff away as I set up the blenders.

Once we made it through the morning rush, I had a window.

"Do you guys mind if I run an errand? I can grab us some lunch?" I offered.

"I'm fine with our boxed lunches," Martha said.

"Me too. Turkey and swiss today. We should start the double chocolate cookies. Come on." Gran shuffled to kitchen with Martha.

"I've got my ear on the bell," Martha reassured.

"Okay, an hour max. I'll be back for lunch," I promised.

I made it to the church early. Mrs. Woodson looked lost in her routine.

I knocked on the partially opened door. "Hi, do you have a minute?"

"Oh, yes, Belle. I'm sorry. It's so quiet these days. I wish they'd pick another pastor. People feel a bit lost watching services from other churches on a screen. But we must have some observation of Sunday or we're not much of a church," Mrs. Woodson said.

"At least they figured out something in the short term. That guy Jeff used to be a pastor," I suggested.

Mrs. Woodson sat up straighter in her dark gray skirt suit. All she was missing was a hat and she'd be straight out of a fifties movie. "The homeless man? I'm not sure that's who we should follow."

"There's an argument that God brought him here. But that's not why I'm here. I wanted to ask who had access to Luke's house," I said.

"Me, the mayor, church council…not that we'd enter while it was occupied. But we all have keys." She smiled.

"That's who has keys. Did anyone have access and was in there? A plumber or painter?" I was grasping at straws, but anyone who got in there once in the right time frame would be a suspect.

"Gus asked too, but the only person in there that I know of, except Luke, is Mrs. Gillis. She cleans the church and the pastor's home. A young widow, no kids and big insurance pay-out. She says it keeps her busy. Normally she goes in Sunday afternoon after service, when he's busy with congregation stuff, or Monday while he's at the market," she explained.

"I'm sure Gus handled it then," I agreed.

"I'm sure. She's not one for snakes or spiders. Nice lady. I can't imagine she'd have any reason or access to a snake like that." Mrs. Woodson shook her head.

"Thanks for the info. I just wanted to be clear on who had access. Do you happen to have her number?" I asked.

Mrs. Woodson opened the drawer of her very tidy desk. "I have her card."

I pulled out my phone and took a picture of her card. "Thanks."

Sitting in my truck, I called Mrs. Gillis and wanted to talk about her cleaning service. She had time, so I headed over to her house.

She was on the fancy side of town in one of those brick ranch-style homes. I parked in front of the house and walked up.

Mrs. Gillis opened the door before I could knock. "Hi, Belle. Come in," she said.

"Hi, Mrs. Gillis. So nice of you to have time. I heard you were the one who keeps the church and Luke's house clean."

"I'm so sorry about your loss, dear," she said.

"Thanks. It didn't work out, but he was a good man." It was always awkward.

Mrs. Gillis gestured for me to sit. Her couches were flower-covered and the side chairs solid. The decoration was nearly Victorian, the colors dark and rich.

"You have a lovely home."

"Thank you. Water? Sweet tea?" she offered.

"No, I'm good. Thank you. I know our sheriff spoke to you about anything you might've seen when cleaning the house," I said.

Her eyes grew. She was short and wiry, but not super-skinny like Mrs. Woodson. She had a matronly quality, that mom feel that would make a child go to her if they got lost at the county fair and needed help.

"Oh, Gus did come by. I didn't see anything. Luke was a bit messy, but not one to leave a door open or food on the floor. Never had ants or beetles around." She shook her head.

"That's good. I just wonder who would do that with a snake? And how they got in." I sighed.

"Well, I'm sure Megan got in somehow. Not that she'd do anything. I felt awful when I found out about that. Not the man I thought he was, but men are weak creatures. Women are the strong ones—men could never take childbirth," she said.

"I haven't had that fun yet, but I've heard." I crossed my arms. "Were there other women?"

"Oh dear, don't torture yourself. He wasn't right for any of you. No one wants a cheater. Pastors have power and people trust them. That can go to their heads. He did do some nice things, though."

"I'd like to hear a nice story," I replied.

"Well, you know how Shelley and her kids up and disappeared?" Mrs. Gillis asked.

I nodded. "I heard her husband was one of the worst."

"Oh yeah, she was always covered up to hide the bruises. Long sweaters in the summer. I liked maxi dresses as much as anyone, but that trended out and she covered her neck with scarves. Some of the older women worried she'd turned Muslim and was going to cover her hair. Of course, she'd never admit it was Ed, but Luke finally spoke to her and offered help," Mrs. Gillis said with a smile.

"She finally took his help. That's great. I hope she's safe," I said.

"Well, it took months. I helped a bit too. Ed wasn't fond of men coming to visit his wife, when he was gone or not. We didn't want Shelley to get beaten for that, so I offered to babysit for free whenever she got a chance to work. Then coming by wasn't so odd. I brought her information, communication from her cousin who had room for her and the kids. We got some donations to get her away, and we talked to some shelters where she'd stay for a few days so he couldn't find her. He didn't know about that cousin, I think. Anyway, I donated money, and Luke and others did." Mrs. Gillis shook her head. "I wish I could know she's okay."

"You did everything you could. It's best no one is in contact with her. But I haven't seen Ed in a long time. I help my friend Katie sometimes at her bar. Ed was there a lot," I explained.

"Not a shock. Nice of you to help your friend. Luke didn't like that, but I think he was too hard on people sometimes. I told him men like Ed don't change. Poor woman has to get out or those kids will be mentally destroyed if not end up dead. I saw the boy with some bruises, and he was a tough little thing, always catching frogs and climbing trees." She dabbed her eyes.

"I'm glad they got away. Can I ask why you have a cleaning business? You seem comfortable."

"Oh, I love cleaning. I just enjoy it. It keeps me fit and I get to see people. A lot of the old people who won't leave their homes need some help. Maybe once a month for the stuff they can't reach on their own. I offered to help your gran when she had that incident, but she was offended, I think," she said.

I smiled. "I'm sure she wasn't, but she's very independent. We are working a lot. I might actually love your help once a month to make sure I'm getting all the areas. Gran and I are at the shop so much."

"I'd be happy to help. Just text me to schedule?" She handed me a card.

"Thanks. Well, I should get back for the lunch rush." I stood and she did as well.

We shook hands and she held my hand a bit longer. "If Ed comes back, you know nothing."

"I understand." I looked her straight in the eye.

"You don't talk to him. You don't try to get anything out of him. He's very dangerous. His wife was terrified of him. A lot of other people are too. Don't get on his radar. You're not an old widow," she warned.

"I understand. I'm not interested in him. If Shelley and the kids are safe, that's all that matters. If she wants to press charges on him, she can do it from wherever she is," I suggested.

"I hope. She might have a problem with those kids." Mrs. Gillis released my hand and walked me to the door.

"What do you mean?" I asked.

"My husband was a lawyer. He worked in family law. You have to prove abuse to a judge to take kids and leave the state. Tennessee tries to keep families close, even if the parents divorce. The parents aren't allowed to move far away without a judge okaying it, not while the kids are young," she explained.

"Well, he'd have to find her to enforce it and there are enough witnesses to testify about the abuse. I hope it doesn't come to that, but all we can do is pray and not stir Ed up," I said.

"Smart girl. Give my best to your grandmother," she said.

"Thank you." I drove back to the shop. Life was so complicated. Love went wrong more often than it seemed to go right. I parked behind the shop because the front spots were all taken. There was a relief in focusing on something I knew was good and would work. Cookies, bread and various pastries—that made people happy.

Mrs. Gillis had been very informative.

Unfortunately, I wasn't any closer to who had killed Luke.

Chapter Fifteen

The last night of class turned out to just be the test and we were out of there in half an hour with temporary cards to prove we'd passed the course and were allowed to serve alcohol in the great state of Tennessee. I dropped Martha at her place and headed to the Buckle.

I parked around back and walked through to the bar. "I'm legit." I put the card on the bar.

There were cheers.

Katie hugged me. "Good for you! When you get the final one, I'll make a proper copy of it for records." She took a picture of the temp card with her phone.

"Need help? Class was just the test," I offered.

"Yeah, the band showed up. I guess something happened — their last venue had a fire, so they turned and came back." Katie filled a tray with orders.

"Want me to call in Martha?" I asked.

"Not yet. My brothers are all here." Katie pointed to the back.

Harry grabbed a tray and grumbled. "She could waitress."

"She's better at the bar. Everyone is on tab, so keep the refills going. I'm going to check on the kitchen," Katie said.

I grabbed a bar towel. "Got it."

I turned to the left side of the bar and, if I'd had a glass in my hand, it would've been shattered on the tile floor. Ed was at the bar and somehow I hadn't noticed him until then.

"Hi, Ed. Refill?" I offered.

"Yep, I ordered cheese fries too. What the hell?" he demanded.

"Katie just went into the kitchen to check." I filled his beer and moved down the bar, checking on everyone.

Then I updated the tabs before I loaded up the pretzel snack bowls on the bar. I kept an eye on Ed so he didn't get grouchy.

Katie came out and served up his fries to more snotty comments.

"Haven't seen you in a while, Ed. Really long haul?" I asked.

"My rig broke down. Own your own truck, they say. You'll make more. But you're also stranded when it needs big repairs. Then I come home and the wife is off somewhere with the kids," he complained.

"Well, glad you got the truck fixed," I said.

"That pastor is lucky he's dead." Ed started to eat.

"What do you mean?" I asked.

"Shel kept saying we should go to him for counseling and stuff. I told her I was too busy and the kids needed her. If he took her side over me, I'd have to talk with him man-to-man." Ed cracked his knuckles.

"Well, Luke is gone. I hope your wife is okay," I said.

"You haven't heard anything?" he asked.

"I'm not a gossip," I shot back.

"Sure, but you hear. Bartenders and coffee bar — you hear stuff," he replied.

I frowned. "I'm not sure it's true. I heard she took them to visit some family since you were on a long haul."

Ed lifted a shoulder. "Probably what she told the choir ladies or the kid's school. I'll find them. She can't last long on her own."

Gus walked in and I felt relief as well as happy to see him.

"I hope it all works out for the best," I said neutrally to Ed.

"Belle. Ed," Gus greeted us as he sat.

"What can I get you, Sheriff?" I asked. "I'm official now."

He admired the card. "Very nice. I won't have to haul you off to jail because someone is counting down your temporary time."

"Lurlene is tracking it on her phone. I'd bet on it," I said.

He chuckled. "The band came back early."

"Something about a fire at the venue. Beer? Water?" I refilled Ed's beer while Gus was chatting.

"She's good." Ed grabbed his glass.

I marked his tab to be sure. Katie came out from the back. "Everything okay?"

I smiled. "Sure. Want me to text Martha?"

"Yes," Harry agreed. "Ordering…"

"I need her for a minute," Gus said.

Katie waved us off as she filled the order, but Megan interrupted everything as she pushed her way to the bar and sat down.

"I need chili cheese fries and a Dr. Pepper, cold," she ordered.

"Damn, who knocked you up?" Ed asked.

The group went silent. Megan's eyes welled up and her lip started to quiver.

"I think he just meant it might be time for some maternity clothes. Don't want to squash the little one. You'll get your figure back in a second when it comes," I reassured her.

"The cravings are just crazy. I can't help it. It's like a little alien took over my body. What do I owe? And don't let me order a second round of fries."

"It's on me." I smiled. "You waitress or bartend before?"

"I waitressed at the diner for a bit. I always end up in a mess," she admitted.

"You're doing okay at the grocery store?"

She nodded. "Martha's mom has a rule. No dating co-workers, which Martha and Harry are probably breaking."

"Well, things happen, but if you have a habit of picking the wrong guys, like I do, it's best not to play where you need to be all business. Katie's been needing some waitressing help. Promise not to date her brothers?" I asked.

"I could use the extra money. I'm trying to save up," she explained.

I looked at Katie. "Fine, I'll give you a try-out tomorrow night. Tonight, if Martha can't come in. Waitress only, and anyone gives you trouble, take it to Harry or Larry."

"You're the best," Megan said. "My ex-husband found out about all this and is trying to get back together. He says he changed."

"I don't think that I ever met him," I said.

"Belle, get that Dr. Pepper, and then we need to check on the kitchen," Katie cut in.

After pouring the drink with extra ice, I followed Katie. "Was that out of line? I just thought it'd be another option for you on the tables. She needs help."

"I know. I don't mind that. I'm just worried about her and customers like Ed. Martha ignores them. I was worried about her too. You need to be a bit tough and sassy to work a bar full of drunk men. She's a mouse," Katie scolded.

"You said the same things about Martha, and now she's working more places with more confidence. Sometimes you have to set a good example and give people a chance to learn. I do feel about bad the maternity clothes remark, but you could park a wheelbarrow in her camel toe. She needs to let that baby breathe," I agreed.

Katie snickered. "True enough. But you're going to staff my bar up into not needing you."

"Never. I prefer behind the bar and I'll always work for free. But you need help with all those tables. Harry isn't good at it," I teased.

"No, and he's full time at the grocery store. Larry works the door well and David can cover. The goal is, Harry is here for fun and just backs up the brothers. But I need a new short-order cook. That one is too slow. Chili fries?" Katie called.

"What's wrong with just fries?" the guy grumbled. "Fries, burgers I got, but heating up chili…"

The microwave dinged and he took out the chili and dumped it on the fries.

"Thanks," I said.

We went back to the bar. "The cook is new."

Katie waved it off. "I hire and fire one a month. Did Martha reply?"

"I'll go outside and call her and see if she's busy." I went around the bar and Gus followed me. "What's wrong?"

"You went to see Mrs. Gillis?" he asked.

"Yeah, she wasn't any major help, but she had access to the house. Is she mad?" I folded my arms and leaned on Gus' SUV.

"No, but she's worried if you keep snooping. She's worried about Ed. I get the idea she helped with Shelley and I just want you to leave Ed and Shelley and all of that alone," he said.

I gave a slight nod. "Okay. I didn't bring it up so much as he did. I asked why he was gone so long."

"Don't ask him anything," Gus instructed.

"We're all just supposed to be afraid of him?" I rolled my eyes.

I heard the door but didn't look. The next thing I remembered was Gus pinning me to his SUV and kissing me until I couldn't breathe and didn't care.

"Way to stake your claim there, Sheriff." Ed whistled. "Make sure to keep her in line."

Gus pulled away. "Shut it, Ed."

I tried to push Gus away. "Women aren't dogs to be trained, Ed."

Ed got into his car and drove off, kicking up gravel. His music was blaring so any response was drowned out. He wouldn't fight me with Gus there.

"Don't mess with him. There's a separate investigation underway and you need to stay out of it," he informed me.

"Fine, but if I was bartending and didn't talk to him at all, it'd be weird. I'll act normal and avoid certain topics."

"Good idea."

"But it wouldn't shock me if he borrowed a motorcycle or rented a car, drove back, planted the snake and left—then he had an alibi no matter what. If the pastor was dead, good. If not, he had a good scare and Ed could finish things when he got back," I added.

"I can't comment on investigations," he said.

I grumbled and texted Martha. "He has a snake tattoo on his arm. Maybe he had snakes as a kid?"

"Belle, please," Gus said.

"Fine, I'm going to help Katie. You playing tonight?"

"Maybe." He pulled me in for another kiss.

I rolled my eyes. "That was quite a display."

"I didn't want Ed to think we were talking about him. Or talking at all," Gus replied.

"But you wanted him to see us making out?"

"He's far less likely to harass you if you're dating me," Gus suggested.

"Men." I sighed. "Are you going to have him pulled over for driving under the influence?"

"I'll make a call to a deputy on duty." Gus grabbed my hand as I turned to go back into the bar.

"What?" I asked.

"You can handle yourself with most people. It's not you."

I shook my head. "I worked in Atlanta, lived there for years."

Gus nodded. "I know. But we don't have Atlanta-level police support or ambulance support here. Cities are different. Small towns, I know people will look after you, Harry and so on, but I don't want anything to happen to you."

"That's sweet, but you're not the boss of me. You can't be with me all of the time."

* * * *

In the middle of the night, nature called, and when I returned to my bed, of course I'd forgotten to fill my water bottle before bed.

I trudged to the kitchen and filled the bottle. With the view from the sink straight out of the back, I saw the sleeping goats and the RV in the distance. The lights were on, but that wasn't a shock. We couldn't hear them, so there was no drama, but I did see a car out there that wasn't familiar.

Gran liked keeping an eye on her property and left her binoculars by the sink to watch out for Duke, missing goats and so on. I debated for a half a second, then grabbed them. I didn't recognize the car, but there was a tent outside. *Probably Jeff. Maybe he got a car on the road?*

Then the door on the RV opened. Someone exited and I had to put the glasses down and rub my eyes. I was awake. I looked again. Sure enough, it was Dina slipping out of there like a cat burglar. I never thought about if they brought girls around to the RV or not. It wasn't my business. But this one, Gus' ex...

The grandfather clock in the dining room struck one.

"Nothing is open after midnight but legs and hospitals." I frowned.

I'd figure out tomorrow who she was seeing. For tonight, I was just grateful something had woken me up to see it. That wasn't going to happen, not on my property.

She drove off and I shook my head.

* * * *

Around lunch the next day, Jeff and the band came. The shop landlord had dropped off the equipment for the improvements and a check for the handyman. They were just glad they didn't have to arrange the repairs. One mention of a code inspection and they were happy to upgrade the electrics. Gran took Jeff into the back while the band got lunch.

The rest of the guys were served, but Dillon had trouble picking a beverage.

"You need to invent a super-caffeinated coffee smoothie," he suggested.

"Late night?" I teased.

"Playing."

"Who was Dina there for?" I asked.

"Do you spy on me, Belle?" Dillon asked.

"No, I got up for some water and saw someone driving away. I recognized her. She's Gus' ex," I explained.

Dillon cocked his head.

"But you know that. Did she try to get you guys to convince Gus to get back together with her?" I asked.

"No, she was getting to know me better. Is that a problem?"

"No, but I don't want her on the property. She's trouble," I replied.

"Those women are the most fun. No offense," Dillon teased.

"None taken. I'm fun, but not 'trailer trash playing with men for rings and running around in the middle of night' fun," I shot back.

Dillon smiled. "I was careful. Thanks for your concern."

"She's so trashy, she best not linger near the curb on garbage day or they'll toss her in," I warned.

"Belle, calm down. We ran into her on the road. She was waitressing. She offered to help. She didn't have anywhere else to go so she rode back with us," he said.

"Where did she go after she left the RV?" I asked.

He shrugged. "I'm not her keeper."

"You need to get rid of her. I don't want her in this town."

"Not very American," he scoffed. "But Gus could help you there."

"Does he know she's back?" I asked.

Dillon nodded. "Not thrilled."

"It's mine and Gran's property. No Dina," I warned.

"Okay, fine. Jeff is okay?" Dillon asked.

"Sure. I'll make you an extra-shot smoothie, but don't blame me if you can't sleep," I warned.

"I won't. Maybe I'll knock on your window?" he teased.

"You'll find a loaded shotgun while you're barking up the wrong tree."

"Wound way too tight and good." He grinned.

"Dina is trouble. I warned you. The only culture that girl will ever have is a yeast infection," I snapped.

"Cat fight." Dillon winked.

I shook my head. "Never. I don't fight over men. I got better things to do. She's the type that'd *only* fight over men. She's a user of men and will trade whatever she's got for it."

"Relax, darlin'. Gus is only interested in you," Dillon reassured.

"I'm not worried about Gus. I don't want Dina taking advantage of Gran or Jeff. They're nice people and might not know about Dina's past." I handed him his extra caffeine.

"Thanks. Good to know. I'm going to catch up the old guys. Milan looks good," Dillon said.

"He just got out of the hospital yesterday, but he swears he's calmer here than at home." At least we could keep an eye on him.

"Probably better than him being home alone, just in case," Dillon pointed out.

It was a creepy feeling as he walked away. The bad girl was always nice deep down in the movies, but was it my business who they were dating? Better Dillon with Dina than her trying to get Gus back. That sounded selfish too. Dillon deserved someone good and not so flighty...but maybe that was what he wanted? What was the word? I didn't know Dina that well, but a lot could be inferred about how she conducted herself on her job and at night.

Gran wouldn't have that behavior on her land, so I knew I was safe warning Dillon. Now I had to ignore this weird tension. Just when I'd started to get ready to date Gus and the feelings were setting in that this could be serious—Dina shows up. It was like driving a shiny new Mercedes off the lot and a bird craps on it...or someone hits it.

Chapter Sixteen

A couple of days later, things almost felt normal. The band was playing and Dina was annoyingly around the bar, but Ed hadn't shown up and that brought down the tension levels to blissfully low.

Jeff sat at the bar, drinking Coke. "I don't mind helping, but RVs and wandering isn't my style. I know the handyman work is nice and I don't mind it, but…"

"You miss preaching?" Katie asked.

Jeff nodded. "I do. But no one is going to hire me."

"Why not? We need one. Something led you here. Why not talk to the mayor and the church board? Worst they could say is no," I replied.

"I thought we have separation of church and state in this country. How do they get away with it?" Jeff asked.

"They are separate as far as authority. Just some leadership crossover. It's a mutual benefits thing—it's the biggest church in town. The mayor is on the church board anyway," Katie added.

I smiled. "We use the church ground and the huge foyer on it for a lot of events for the town. Instead of having a separate community center or a church food pantry and a town food pantry, we have one combined. The town helps with some of the upkeep of the grounds and outside. The town voted on it years ago. People got mad their taxes were paying for something and the church was doing it too, so they were paying twice."

"Slippery slope," Jeff agreed.

"Exactly, but it's a tiny town, so it works if the lines and rules are clear. I think Luke liked to take advantage of his position too much," Katie commented.

"We need someone who's seen life's challenges, not just been picked and raised to be a pastor and life handed it to him," I agreed.

Jeff sipped his Coke. "Some people like believing their pastor is above things. Is better."

"Those are judgy people. The ones who need help feel better knowing we're all human." Katie shook her head. "Plenty of people didn't like a single young woman buying a bar. *What will people think?*"

I laughed. "It's true. But she's good at it. Her brothers look out for trouble. What does it matter if she's married or not? I remember one woman saying at least if she was a widow it'd be better."

Jeff chuckled. "Women are supposed to be perfect while men can sow their oats. It's a double standard I don't support."

"If men can fool around, but women can't, what women are they having fun with?" Katie asked.

Dina flirted with the band and was keeping far away from me. I nodded to her.

Katie smiled. "She is exactly...look at those heels. Those are stripper high heels."

"Higher the heels, the lower the morals," I sassed.

Jeff smiled at us. "Maybe I will go speak to the mayor and church board."

Gus walked in and it was tense. Dillon approached him, but Gus waved off playing today. Dina didn't dare.

"Is it weird?" Gus asked as he sat down.

"Oh, no, not at all. Dina and I are like two peas in a pod. Thick as thieves. No ax to grind except I want her gone," I demanded.

"I'll see what I can do," Gus replied.

"I'll help," Jeff offered.

"First, I need to ask you something. Megan was around Luke a lot. He never talked to you about her?" Gus asked Jeff.

Jeff frowned. "He talked about Belle a bit. He said another woman was complicated and didn't work out. Obviously, the damage was done. Maybe they didn't know about the pregnancy, but it didn't seem to bother Luke."

"She said her ex was protective and concerned. Hopefully she won't go through it all alone. Have you tracked him down?" I asked Gus.

He consulted his notebook. "He's in the army, not deployed, but he's accounted for on the weekend in question. That doesn't mean he couldn't have had someone do it as a scare tactic."

"The army is probably what broke them up. Very hard for spouses to move around to army housing away from their families and some support system," Jeff said.

The suspect list was getting really short. Those with true motives were almost gone. Megan's ex getting someone to plant the snake was possible.

"Where's Ed?" Gus asked.

"Hasn't shown up today," I replied.

"Makes a nice change. He wasn't here yesterday either. We should pray he's on another long haul," Katie teased.

I sipped a Diet Coke. "I'm worried he's after Shelley. That man lies like a no-legged dog. Can't we get her a warning?"

Gus shook his head. "I spoke to Mrs. Gillis, but she dropped Shelley off somewhere and someone else picked her up. There's a way to do these things so no one knows everything. No one can expose her."

"I just wish we could warn her. A call or something, do you think maybe she called Luke to let him know she's safe? Maybe from a neighbor's phone or a new burner phone?" I asked.

"I did have some phone numbers on Luke's phone that weren't contacts and left no messages. It's possible she called and he picked up. I assumed they were robocalls," Gus dismissed.

"You didn't check them?" I nudged.

"They are being run, but things take time, Belle. It's not a TV show. He blocked the contacts but didn't delete the call or numbers from his history. If they were something he'd be afraid someone would see, he would've deleted them. I went through all the deleted stuff first. We'll get the info back soon and see what it says," Gus assured.

"You only found one phone at Luke's?" I asked.

Katie cleared her throat. "Belle, why don't you and the sheriff go take a walk around the bar, check the back? We're pretty packed today and I don't want anyone acting dumb in the parking lots."

"Isn't that what your brothers are for?" I teased.

"Come on." Gus waved at me.

A break sounded good, so I followed him out of the front and we walked slowly through the rows of cars.

"You think it's worth tracking her down?" Gus asked.

"She's the only suspect we haven't been able to rule out."

"She wasn't here. She's been in hiding."

"But she has friends too. Family enough to take her in. It's possible someone wanted to be sure Luke would stay away," I suggested.

"We're running them all down. I just can't believe Shelley would do that after what Luke did to help...even if he did get some things very wrong. Cutting off contact and moving on is one thing. Why harm Luke?" he asked.

I caught up to him and whispered, "Ed. What's more dangerous than stepping on the tail of a two-headed rattler? An abuser who has gotten away with it for years and is so cocky he sat on a barstool and said he'd find his family. He'd have a talk with Luke, and he didn't mean a nice friendly chat. Ed didn't have a flinch of remorse. He doesn't care if we all know what he is."

Gus nodded. "He's dangerous, but he's smart enough to get people dependent on him first. The guy doesn't start a ton of bar fights, unpleasant as he is."

"I still say he could've sent someone to deal with Luke. If Megan's ex could've, why not Ed?" I asked.

Gus smiled at me. "Because Ed's sort of friends would've left ten snakes and Luke would've been tied up naked covered in mice."

I laughed. "That's a visual I didn't need."

"If it was Ed behind it, the job would be done."

"Really? He might be smart, but not every trucker is. Maybe there were more snakes and they got away," I suggested.

"Agreed." Gus sighed.

"I say Shelley is behind it. She got someone or hired them to take Luke out and make it look accidental, if possible."

"Why would she hurt the guy who helped her?" Gus asked.

"Because deep down, Luke was mostly a selfish coward. He helped people when it was safe for him. Mrs. Woodson and Mrs. Gillis know about it. Which means half of the PTA at the kids' school will. Why do you think Ed suspects Luke? Marriage counselling and all of that is a good cover, but he knows his wife was talking to Luke. The longer she's gone with no contact, the more he'd suspect Luke. If Luke is dead, Ed might not have a trail to follow. Luke couldn't help but brag about what he did, unofficially," I warned.

"Shelley would be grateful," Gus said.

"And still be scared out of her mind. Men like Ed won't stop, ever. She's got his kids. Legally, he's got a right to see them, until a judge says different because of the abuse. If she called Luke to say she's okay, even from a truck stop so old it still has pay phones — that could be used to track her. Luke wouldn't take a beating from Ed," I argued.

"He'd give up the info." Gus nodded.

"Faster than an idiot running after he mowed over a yellow jacket nest or a hooker in church." I looked around. Only a few couples making out. Nothing like drug deals or hookers working the area. "Should we go in?"

He leaned over and kissed me. "I have to go."

"Why? Don't avoid the Buckle on account of Dina. She gives white trash a bad name and it shows ten times worse in a decent bar," I mocked.

He smiled. "Not her. I gotta track those numbers and locate Shelley best I can. Maybe I'll get the Tennessee Bureau involved."

I shook my head. "Don't bother. Mrs. Gillis said something. I think they went out of state."

Gus cocked his head at me. "Which one?"

"You should check with her to be sure, but I think they went a tiny bit north is all. I better go help." I kissed his cheek.

"State lines make things harder," Gus reminded.

"Harder for you, safer for her. I didn't make any of these choices. Don't give me the sour puss." I wagged a finger at him. Who could blame a mom protecting her kids? The laws protected keeping the kids in close contact with both parents, so she'd have to prove her hubby was abusive to block his rights. That'd hurt the kids. He's their dad, evil or not, and they'd end up blaming their mom instead of the court.

I knew who I was praying for in church on Sunday. People could make fun of my parents for running off, but when I saw situations like Shelley's, I was grateful I hadn't gotten stuck in a dysfunctional or abusive relationship. Gran and Grandpa had loved each other and me, and no one had gotten hit unless it was smacking my hand away from the stove or a fancy cake frosted to perfection. And those hadn't even hurt.

"Belle, bar's getting backed up," Larry called.

"Coming." I jogged to the back door. "Where's Martha?"

"Out with Harry on a Nashville date." Larry rolled his eyes.

"Okay, we'll text Megan in to cover tables," I said. "But Martha and Harry are cute."

Larry smiled. "She's nice."

I walked in to a fussy crowd and a dead keg. I immediately started pouring shots and sliding bottled beers to those with empty glasses. "I'm busier than a one-armed paper hanger, so everyone just show the manners your mama gave y'all."

* * * *

Between Gus, Mrs. Gillis, Mrs. Woodson and some of Shelley's family in Tennessee, Gus managed to figure out where in Kentucky she might be hiding.

It was a weird date, but I'd packed lunch and we had a few hours to talk. We never ran out of conversation or argued seriously.

"Are you sure it's her?" I asked.

"She bought a used car under her maiden name," he said.

"Stupid," I muttered.

"She had to buy something. Shelley isn't a criminal. She doesn't want to break the law. It makes her much easier to find." Gus shrugged.

Before we got near Shelley's, we made a pit stop and had a picnic on the squad car.

"Gran doing better?" he asked.

"She needs her routine. Emergencies like when Milan had the heart attack just throw her off more. She doesn't eat the same, take her meds at the same time and all the stress…"

"What are you going to do?" he asked.

"Martha is working all day at the shop today and we should be home for dinner. But Martha is taking her girls over to Gran's to play with the goats. I've also spoken to Mrs. Gillis. She's not even fifty — really young widow. I'm going to have her come clean once or twice a month to start. Places it's too hard to get or we haven't had time to go over."

"Your gran will hate it," Gus said.

I nodded. "At first, but when she realizes Mrs. G is a widow just like her — looking for something to do, like Gran with her shop — I think she'll feel better about it. A little time and Gran will be comfortable with Mrs. G in the house. That way, if something comes up, I can ask Mrs. G to stay with Gran. Or help her throughout a day when I can't be there, at the shop or wherever. We're busier than a raccoon in tall corn some days, so I need backup. Not that Gran needs medical caretaking, just someone to keep her on track when her routine is totally backwards. Am I crazy?"

He shook his head. "Not at all. That's smart. Martha and Katie have to work. We'd all help, but Mrs. Gillis has the most flexible schedule. Her hubby left her well set enough to work when or really if she wants to."

"I don't ever want Gran to feel like I'm pawning her off, but I can't be in two places at once." I'd thought I'd be her shadow once I moved home, but we weren't conjoined twins. Sometimes the world was going to drag us in different directions for a bit.

"She'd never think that. You know it's not true. Life happens. I couldn't have done this without you," he said.

"I do feel like I need to be there. If she's surrounded by all men, that could be very scary for her," I pointed out.

"Kentucky state troopers are sending a female deputy and a female social worker. She'll have to be processed here and handed over. Depending on whether she denies or admits anything, it might take days or weeks to get them to hand her over." He shrugged.

"We don't have any female deputies," I observed.

"I'm open to it, but small southern towns... Good ole boys in bar fights need to be wrestled apart and such. A little lady like you couldn't do it," Gus teased.

"Whack 'em in the business with a full bottle. That always worked fine in Atlanta." I grinned.

"You were security?" he asked.

"No, but do you know how long it takes to get Atlanta PD to show up? Big city, lots of murders and everything. A bar brawl isn't at the top of the list. Hotel bars especially, since we have security, but a two-man fight turns into a mob. You have catch that before it grows like weeds. I've a couple tricks up my sleeve."

"I can't wait to hear, but we should get going." He tossed our trash into the can as I settled into the car.

Another twenty minutes and we pulled up to a trailer.

Two kids were playing outside, but they ran in when they saw the cop car. Gus knocked on the door.

"Shelley, it's me. We need to talk," Gus said.

I wondered how many times Gus had been out to try and help Shelley. He could press charges on Ed, but if Shelley kept letting Ed back into the house or never moved out... I wouldn't want Gus' job for the world.

The door opened and Shelley looked healthier than she ever had. Not so frail and shaky.

"Come on in, I guess," she invited.

"Hi," I said.

"Eddie, Christy, you remember Miss Belle and Sheriff Gus?" Shelley asked.

"Hi," the kids replied in unison.

"Go play in the bedrooms. Grown-ups have to talk," Shelley explained.

Eddie was about ten and went into one room. Christy was only about five and headed into the other bedroom.

"How did you find me?" Shelley asked as she sat on the flea market couch.

"You bought a car under your maiden name. Registered it to this address. Your family did a good job of dodging any questions," Gus acknowledged.

"I called a friend from high school. He owns the trailer park. Had this hunk of junk empty and he's letting me stay for free. But I needed a car to get some work. I don't want to break the law, Sheriff. I want to be safe and my kids to be safe," she insisted.

"Self-defense is nature's oldest law. We're not here about you running. We know what you were going through," I assured her.

"Ed is still determined to find you, so be aware of that. We're here about Luke's murder," Gus warned.

"Murder? I've cut off all contact. I have no idea what happened," she said.

"He was strangled to death by a python. I know you called Luke when you got safe. I tracked the call to a diner about forty miles from here. If I can do it, it's possible Ed could've gotten info out of Luke," Gus said.

"You think Ed killed Luke? It's possible, to get info, but he'd use his fists, not a snake," Shelley chuckled.

A bedroom door creaked shut.

Shelley waved it off. "The doors don't stay closed. The whole trailer is all catawampus."

"Mind if I talk to Eddie?" I asked.

She fumbled for a tissue. "I guess. He's still a boy. I kept him from stuff."

I walked down the hall and tapped on his door. "Eddie, can we talk?"

He opened the door and I saw it. Or rather, them!

The hissing was hard to escape. All around the room were glass enclosures with reptiles of all sorts. "Wow, Mrs. Gillis said you were into frogs, but you've got all kinds here."

"Yep. Want to help feed them?" Eddie asked.

"Could I? Thanks." It was probably a great honor, but I would've happily declined.

"Snakes aren't bad like people say. They're just different. Sort of scary, but they only have their mouths to protect them," he said with a smile.

I nodded. "Did you have a lot of snakes back in Sweet Grove?"

He frowned and his shoulders sank three inches. "I had to let them all go. Mom said we couldn't take them. I had to catch a whole new set of pets."

"Well, it's a very impressive collection. I see rattlers and cottonmouths." I looked around and wanted to run.

"Here. Grab a mouse by the tail and toss it in. Be quick." Eddie put his hand on the lid of the snake enclosure.

I opened the shoebox marked *mice*, expecting one to jump out at me. They were dead, if not mostly dead. I quickly grabbed one tail and closed the box. This was a trust thing. I got it. Eddie didn't trust a lot of people.

"Ready? He's hungry. One, two, toss," Eddie instructed.

I tossed and the snake caught the mouse in the air. Eddie closed the lid and I could breathe again.

"You're cool. Not like some girls. Do you know anyone who has a python?" he asked.

Python?

"No, I don't know anyone who has a collection anywhere near yours. Pythons aren't native here though, right?" I asked.

"Right. You're smart. That's why I need someone who has one. I got my last one from a kid in high school. His family was moving away and his parents wouldn't let him take his collection. He released the native stuff, but the exotic ones were too dangerous. I got a free snake." He finished the feeding. "Here I clean out the mice traps around the trailers. Some people give me some cash for it, but at least it's free food."

"I don't see a python. What happened to your python when you had to move so fast?" I asked.

He sat on the bed and looked at his shoes. "I left it for a friend, but I don't think he liked it. He probably got rid of it."

"What friend?" I asked.

He shot me a look that scared me a bit. "It's Pastor Luke's fault. We had a house and a dad. Now we're in a trailer and it barely has anything in it. The heat won't work. I knew we'd be worse off. Dad told me if we ever had to leave, it'd be worse."

"I'm sorry it's worse, but I heard your dad could be mean." I had to be careful.

Eddie nodded. "Yeah. Why do you think I kept a bunch of snakes? He thought I was badass. I told Mom, if it got too bad, I wouldn't feed the snakes for a while so they were starving. We'd wait for Dad to come home drunk…then guide him into my bedroom. I'd dump some dead mice on him and then pull the lids off. We'd lock the door behind us and brace it with something.

They'd attack him for sure. That many venomous bites and a python? Then we'd lie to the cops. Say that Dad went into the wrong room because he was drunk. I wasn't there because I'd slept with my sister. She got scared Dad wasn't home yet." Eddie batted his big innocent eyes that any judge would believe.

"Wow. Why didn't you?" I asked.

"Mom wouldn't. She told me that was wrong. Pastor Luke was going to help. But Dad was right. This is worse. Is Pastor Luke really dead?" Eddie asked.

"You left your python with Luke?" I asked.

Eddie shook his head. "Not really. I left it with a guy at school. I told him to wait until Sunday service and slip the snake into the pastor's house. Put it in the closet or something. It was a surprise, but he'd like it. He wanted the snake."

"Your friend believed that?" I asked.

"Never said he was my friend. I wasn't sure he'd do it. Maybe he'd keep it or try to sell it. But he was always getting in trouble during Sunday school. Especially when Pastor Luke taught it. He loved the idea of a prank. It's just a snake. Not even venomous," Eddie replied.

"Eddie, you know how pythons kill their prey, right?" Gus asked. I hadn't heard him come in.

"Duh, pythons crush. Wind around a mouse and squeeze." Eddie mimicked being squeezed.

"How did your classmate at school handle the snake?" Gus asked.

"His dad does those roundups when there are too many rattlers. He had a stick where you can clamp the head, sort of. Or behind the head. Works good on the venomous ones. Pythons, you gotta control the body too. But the kid helped his dad at roundups so he was used to it," Eddie explained.

"What guy does roundups in our town?" I asked.

"Oh, his dad doesn't live with him. He goes out to the east end of Tennessee where his daddy works now. Divorce. But he did so well at a roundup that his daddy gave him his very own snake stick and a canvas bag to hold 'em in." Eddie sounded envious.

"That sounds really cool, but snakes are dangerous," I commented.

Eddie nodded. "I know. I'm careful. Never got bit. My sister never got bit either. I'd kill the snake that did that."

Gus knelt down and looked Eddie in the eye. "Eddie, your python squeezed Pastor Luke to death."

Eddie sighed, but there was a twinkle in his eyes. "It's his own fault, then."

"What?" I asked.

"He made us move. He said he'd help us. I couldn't let that snake go in the wild. That'd be wrong. The least Pastor Luke could've done was help him find a new home. He wasn't a bad snake. If you fed him, he was like a lap dog." Eddie folded his arms.

"Eddie?" Shelley asked through her tears.

"I didn't mean for the snake to kill him." Eddie tucked his chin into his chest. "Snakes are animals. They follow their instincts."

Gus got down on Eddie's level. "Did your friend have anything to do with slipping snakes into local businesses? Maybe like a decoy?"

Eddie shrugged. "Maybe. He liked the attention."

"How are you in contact with this boy?" Shelley demanded.

"Duh, social media. I created a fake account. I can go to the library or log on from your tablet. It doesn't have my name or any information," Eddie replied.

"Kids and technology," I acknowledged.

"Were you in contact with your dad?" Shelley asked.

Eddie shook his head. "No, I was hoping Trevor left a snake in his place, but he said it'd be too obvious. It would've been easier than scaring or hurting Luke."

Shelley shook her head. "Luke is dead and he helped us."

"I had a better plan using my own pets that Dad let me have, but cuz I'm a kid, no one listens. Now Pastor Luke is dead and Daddy will come for us. Then it'll be worse," Eddie said through the big tears of a kid being brave.

"We won't let that happen," Gus promised.

"Promises don't mean jack. Kids know a liar," Eddie said.

I wiped away a tear.

Shelley hugged her son. "I swear, I won't let him hurt you."

"I won't let him hurt me or Christy. I told him, he touches us and he'll find water moccasins in his boots. He can throw out my whole collections, I'll find more. I'll fill his rig full of snakes. I can and I will." Eddie broke down sobbing on his mother's shoulder.

"Eddie, if you tell the judge how bad it is, he can block your daddy from seeing you," I suggested.

Shelley and Eddie both chuckled through their tears.

"Ed isn't afraid of courts or jail," Shelley warned.

Eddie sniffled and wiped a tear away with a fist. "He'd kill us all if he thought he couldn't hold on. I'm not mean or dumb. We had to get away or he had to die."

"Why didn't you leave the python in the trailer for your dad to find?" I asked.

Eddie frowned and scratched his head. "I don't know. One snake...he'd probably do okay with that one. Luke would be terrified. It was funnier. I hope I didn't get Trevor in trouble. It's not like he programmed the snake to be mean or anything."

Gus pulled Shelley and me out of the bedroom. "I'm going to have a word with the Kentucky trooper, and social workers will come in and interview Eddie. He might get some counseling or a little time in a juvenile facility. I'll have a talk with Trevor and his parents when I get back, too."

"Juvy? No, my baby was trying to protect us. Maybe play a bad joke on the pastor, but murder wasn't the intent," she insisted.

"A judge will decide that, but you'll probably end up back in Tennessee. You can't move that far away from your kid's father without a Tennessee judge signing off on your agreement," Gus explained. "I'm sorry."

"Me too. I never thought..." I put my hand over my mouth to avoid saying the wrong thing.

"We finally had a shot," Shelley said.

Gus put a hand on her shoulder. "You need to go through the courts. Divorce, document the abuse. I'll testify. Plenty of people will. Once you've proven he's an abuser, you can go as far away as you want. I'm sure people will help you raise some money to move. The key is you need to stand your ground and fight him in court. Make him pay."

Shelley sighed. "I don't have a choice. I'll get the kids to pack up."

When she opened Eddie's door, the window was open.

"He's gone." Shelley stared. "His emergency backpack too."

"He can't have gotten that far," Gus advised. He ran out to inform the other troopers.

Epilogue

Milan was back with the crew in the shop and acting like a supervisor as Jeff and Gus fixed the wiring. I tried very hard not to pay attention to the cursing coming from the back.

"So little Eddie was found and isn't going to jail?" Martha asked as she stocked the preserves.

"He's a child. It was a prank," Gran argued.

"Or maybe he wanted Luke to take care of the snake since he couldn't release it? But they had to leave so fast he didn't get a chance to do it right," Milan argued.

"The kids are victims of their dad's abuse, and having to leave like that—I feel sorry for them, but you don't leave a deadly snake in someone's house," I argued.

"But, Belle, kids don't think things through," Martha explained.

"He had a plan to handle his father. But you're right. Kids don't think things through the same way as adults." I blended my berry smoothie until it was the perfect shade of blue.

"That's why they shouldn't be allowed to keep dangerous animals as pets. They could end up in the hospital or worse." Gran fussed over the coffee pots as the power blinked.

"You ladies should be good to go," Jeff announced.

"A pastor shouldn't be doing that sort of work," Gran said.

"Happy to help. I'm only on trial for a few months," Jeff admitted.

"People liked your few weeks' try-out. Like the pastor's house?" I asked.

Jeff smiled. "Better than the jail or a closet, but I keep an eye out for snakes."

"What happened to Eddie?" Milan asked Gus.

"He and his friend in town who actually put the snake in the house both got probation for a few years and can't own any dangerous pets while on probation," Gus said.

"And Shelley?" Martha asked.

"That's a longer process. She's given testimony about the abuse, supplied the court with pictures and also filed for divorce. Obviously, she has a restraining order, but she had to move back to Tennessee for the court. She's staying with family. Ed is pissed and dangerous." Gus poured himself an ice water.

"Making yourself at home?" I teased.

We'd been on a few dates since our Kentucky road trip. *So far, so good, except when Dina crashes the fun at the Buckle.*

Gus' phone beeped and he checked it.

"I got the land with the trailer. They have to inspect and then we'll close, but it's all accepted and approved. Can't get rid of me now, neighbor," Gus teased.

Gran clapped her hands. "Oh good, he has a barbed wire fence along his perimeter. We can let the goats roam farther. We won't charge you for grass trimming services."

I laughed. "Gran."

"What? Now you boys go on to the house and put up those enclosures for the goats on our side. Took forever getting them in," Gran huffed.

"I think Lurlene has something to do with that. Sounded like they were there but no one called to set up a time for me to pick them up." I shook my head.

"Neighbors?" Martha asked with a teasing innuendo in her voice.

"I wanted a bit more land and to still be in town. It's better than renting and a start." Gus smirked.

Before the debate on financing and the housing market could begin, the band entered like royalty. Dillon and the guys ordered smoothies and muffins, and paid.

"You guys gotta come tonight. Three new songs. Gus better sit in," Troll said.

"If they're new, I don't know them," Gus countered.

"That's deep. We'll teach you." Troll smiled.

"Gus doesn't have to if he doesn't want to. He's got a steady girlfriend and an annoying ex. His life is complicated," Dillon teased.

"You're the one who brought her back here," I snarked.

"Free country, she can go where she wants. Not on your property, we got that part," Dillon said.

"The enclosures came in for the goats, if you want to help," Gran suggested.

"We're on that. Heading back right now." Troll nodded to Jeff's tool belt. "Is Pastor Jeff going to help?"

"You coming to church on Sunday?" Jeff asked.

Troll shrugged. "Can't hurt. I hear your services are cool. Talking, not scolding or harsh. When I was a kid, church was nothing but sit still, itchy clothes and going to hell."

"I try to avoid all of those things. There are lot of pretty ladies in church." Jeff smiled. "Let's go build stuff. Idle hands…"

Troll laughed. "I remember that. Idle hands are the devil's workshop. I learned to play music and my hands always have something to do."

"Maybe you could take a look at the oven at the Buckle? It's slower than all get out. Might need a new one, but something is wrong. We cleaned the grease trap and the vents, but nothing. I want to create a new menu for the bar—apps and so on, but it's no good if the oven is unreliable," Martha worried.

"We'll be there tonight before the guys go on," Jeff offered.

"Thanks," Martha said.

"I'm good with appliances. Gotta have cold beer," Troll joked.

* * * *

That night, Gran was out to dinner with her fellas while Gus and I were trying out the apps Martha had whipped up. It took Jeff ten minutes and a new part from the store to fix the oven.

"These are great, Martha!" I gushed.

"Yes, I'm going to gain ten pounds just nibbling in my own bar." Katie stuffed her face again.

"Wouldn't hurt you. Ladies today are too skinny," Jeff said. "I'm off."

"Stay for the band," Troll encouraged.

Katie's cheeks were a bit pink. "Yeah, I owe you a drink at least."

Jeff sat down and ordered a Coke. He looked a lot younger after a haircut, shave and some new clothes. He couldn't be more than forty.

Lurlene strolled in and ordered a drink.

"Glad they had that part in at the store, Miss Lurlene," Jeff said.

"We can order whatever you need, pastor. No trouble at all," she said.

Martha smiled. "You might have enough room for a new pizza oven, Katie. Expand your business. Put in a carryout window. Maybe delivery service?"

"Maybe." Katie shrugged.

"To small towns and small business," Jeff said.

We all lifted our glasses and toasted.

The band began to set up. I looked at Gus. "You're not going to go join in?"

"Nah. You?" he asked.

I shook my head. "I don't like singing in public."

"You disapprove of the choir?" Jeff asked.

"No, it's not that sort of singing and Gran never liked young ladies make a spectacle of themselves," I explained.

Jeff took a deep breath. "Gifts aren't meant to be withheld."

"People are awful hard to please. Being in the spotlight just gives them a chance to nitpick," I replied.

Lurlene turned back from the stage and sampled a loaded potato wedge from our plate. "Don't you worry. It looks like Dina is helping them tonight."

I glanced over and shrugged. Gus didn't say a word.

With the murders solved in Sweet Grove, now I could turn my attention to how to get rid of pests like Dina and figure out how to keep Lurlene from meddling in things. At least I had a hunky new neighbor and things were on the right path for us...

"We need to add a hot fudge sundae to your menu," I suggested.

Katie laughed. "You supply me with some frozen hot fudge smoothies and I sell them."

"Done," I agreed.

That sounded like a delicious next project...

A Note from Belle

Hey y'all,

I can't even begin to believe it was a kid…but given his plan for his daddy and who his daddy is, that kid is going to be in jail at some point or another. Hopefully this chance for probation and guidance will get him on the right track for a different life. I'd bet my life and my truck his dad, Ed, will get himself behind bars soon, but the family might be safer.

Not that my old truck is worth much these days…

Don't you worry about Dina. Katie and I will figure something out. The goats are too precious for words, but I'm not sure I can use them to get rid of Dina or sell enough of them to buy me a proper and new-to-me used truck.

I do have a new neighbor coming and we've got a new pastor, who I think we'll all like better. If he can get Troll to come to church, maybe he'll surprise us all.

Don't forget to come back for my hot fudge sundae smoothie and the berry blues. I can't tell which is better…

Appreciate cha!

Belle

Want to see more like this?
Here's a taster for you to enjoy!

A Little Bit Cupid: Lovestruck
January Bain

Excerpt

Emma Valentine Hurst's hand hovered over the open chocolate box. Hmm. *A sinfully dark chocolate truffle or a heart-shaped melt-in-my-mouth orange liquor?* After her dismal morning, both.

She slipped the first one into her mouth, closed her eyes and let it melt on her tongue while trying to ignore the ongoing struggle of wills between mother and son right behind her. A sudden, sharp snap alerted her to trouble. She whirled around to discover her new Cupid-with-arrow display teetering precariously on its pedestal. In a flash, she leapt the short distance, just in time to save the display from toppling over, but not in time to stop the child from taking off with his prize, clutched in his candy-stained hands—the bow and arrow recently held upright and loaded for action by none other than Cupid himself.

"Timmy! Stop that! Put that back right now. Don't you dare, young man, I'm warning you!"

Timothy Adam Jones took off like a bat right out of, well, Hades for the front door of the newly minted Valentine's Candy Shoppe, his mother Vanity trying desperately to catch up with the five-year-old. He seemed to have been blessed with feet that must be invisibly winged like Mercury or Hermes, depending on whether one preferred the Romans or the Greeks. Emma was personally more enamored of the Greeks, as their mythology came first, though Cupid was decidedly more Roman.

But the determined child, who had already made the front entrance, also had the advantage of being sugar-fueled, thanks to his doting mother allowing him to graze at each and every candy bin to his heart's content, hence Emma's dismal morning. To Vanity's credit, she was hampered by her four-inch heels, a tight pencil skirt and a multitude of hair extensions that obscured her sideways vision like blinders on a plow horse. The fashion plate succeeded in only teetering dangerously back and forth on the tiled floor and within precarious inches of a towering display of cut-glass crystal stemware.

Emma swallowed the remains of the chocolate and charged after the child, waving off his mother, who gave her a grateful, though chagrined, look. After all, he had *her* Cupid's arrow clutched in his tight little fists, having torn it from *her* new Valentine's display. So now the display didn't make sense, for why would Cupid be holding his arms out so awkwardly? Pretending to *mime* an arrow? It just wasn't going to work.

And not to mention that her best friend Charm McCall had loaned it to her with the express order that Emma keep it safe and out of anyone's hands. That it was the real deal. And, knowing Charm, that meant it was charged with magic, whatever that would entail. But right now, all Emma wanted was to get the precious artifact back in one piece and where it belonged before her friend found out what had happened.

Timmy turned the handle of the shop's front door and slipped through the opening before she could grasp the back of his snowsuit.

"Whoopee, I'm Robin Hood!" he yelled at the top of his surprisingly robust lungs while tearing off down the street, holding his prize in front of him.

Emma took off after him, grateful for her running shoes. She ignored the frosty air that bit at her skin. February in Snowy Lake in the northern reaches of Canada's heartland was a cold, cold affair. The next two weeks plus one day of celebrating the Winter Festival — claim to fame the longest one in Canada, beating out Quebec by twenty-four hours — concluded with a Valentine's Dance on Saturday, February fourteenth. *The town, competitive? Naw. Well, maybe.* But it was the highlight of their winter and helped the residents, all twelve hundred and fifty-nine of them on a good day, beat the doldrums of the endless, freezing white stuff that lined driveways and fields with equal abandon. *Snow. The four-letter word that was greeted with such fanfare in late October, and vilified by most by early February.*

"Timmy! Stop! I'll give you a big bag of candy," she yelled at the small figure disappearing down the street, doing a dazzling display of male daring by pretending to shoot every person he met. He was also too busy darting around the legs of passersby to pay her any mind. *She began to gain on him. Just a few more steps and I'll have that little candy monster in my grasp.*

Ah-ha. She reached for him just as he let the arrow loose from the bow. *No!* She watched in horror as it went flying into the air on a straight trajectory and right into the backside of a retreating figure. The person, a man, stopped in his tracks. *Oh – fudge.* He was walking alongside Charm's Mountie, Ace Collins. She grabbed the bow from Timmy and clutched it to her stomach. The child slumped to the sidewalk and began to cry.

The tall man, as tall as Ace—who Charm had likened to Bigfoot on first meeting him out at Saskatoon, berry picking, last fall—turned around and stared right at her. Everyone else backed away a bit, leaving them to sort it out. Of course, they all stayed, lining the sidewalk—a good show in Snowy Lake was not something to be missed. A popcorn vendor was likely on his way.

"You could have just said hello, but I get your point," the man said, his brown eyes locked with hers. She couldn't seem to find her tongue to speak. *Words. That's what's needed.* He'd just said something clever, so now it was her turn. But what could she say to this fine-looking hunk of maleness who carried such a striking resemblance to the town's newest Mountie? Right down to the rich brown, wavy hair and chiseled jawline. *Oh. My. Goddess.*

"I'm sorry. It wasn't me. I mean, it's my bow, on loan, but I didn't shoot you. Timmy, tell the man." She looked in desperation at the young boy still carrying on his now full-blown tantrum at her feet, rolling around the sidewalk in his bright blue snowsuit. "Tell him *you* shot him in the—aw—derrière, not me."

No help in that direction. Timmy ignored everything but his own grief at the loss of his new toy. The man continued to stare at her for a few more intense seconds, eyebrows raised in disbelief, before seeming to realize he had an arrow attached to his backside. Ace, his ever-supportive brother, stopped laughing long enough to inspect the damage.

"Afraid we're going to need medical intervention, Stone. That thing's rather well embedded." Ace's tone was quite calm for a man whose sibling had just been shot.

"Just pull it out already!" Stone's deep voice growled from inside his rather large chest. He wore a black leather jacket and a navy-blue wool scarf wrapped around his neck. *Too bad the jacket isn't a longer length. It would have better protected his, ah – assets.*

"If you're sure?" Ace did the honors. Emma stood frozen to the spot, in plain sight of the full-face wince that came over Stone's handsome features as the arrow was withdrawn from the back pocket of his blue jeans, courtesy of his brother. She tried not to stare, but the removal of the arrow left a hole dead center of the pocket, though surprisingly no blood. *Huh.*

Ace handed her the arrow. "You might want to keep better control of this." He didn't look too concerned, a twinkle lurking in his eyes as per usual. He was of great value to the town. A good man who knew his job and had the smarts to be pairing off with her best friend. His brother took a few more seconds before joining them. Emma swallowed over the lump in her throat. Even though she should be freezing in just a blouse and pants, perspiration trickled down her underarms.

"Stone, I'd like you to meet Emma Valentine Hurst, the new owner of the Valentine's Candy Shoppe. Emma, meet my younger brother Stone, who's up to visit for a couple of weeks."

She looked up, way up now that he was standing so close, and into deep brown eyes that matched the lovely color of melting chocolate, she decided in the moment. He removed his glove and offered his hand.

She took it, a spark of electricity zinging right through her whole body as their hands touched. It made her jump and she tried to pull her hand away. But he held on, his smile widening. His eyes gleamed with some kind of devilment.

"Lovely to meet you, Miss Emma Valentine Hurst." Even the way he spoke the harmless greeting took her breath away.

"Ah, thanks, nice to meet you. I'm sorry about what happened." No need to mention all the facts.

"If it hadn't happened, I wouldn't have had the pleasure of standing here right now speaking to such a pretty lady."

Ace looked bemused. Actually, kind of flummoxed was more like it. He took off his Stetson and thrust a hand through his hair, then placed his hat back on his head. There was an odd twist to his lips. Had something else happened she wasn't party to? He looked full of something.

"Anything I can do to make it up to you, please, like free chocolates, or anything, just ask. My store's just down the block." She forced herself to look away and deal with Timmy, who had finally stopped his over-the-top caterwauling. She helped the child to his feet and held on tight to his hand, making sure the bow was well away from temptation.

Out of the corner of her eye, she saw her friend Charm come flying out of the Tea & Tarot café. In mere seconds, she joined them, holding one hand over her chest to ease the sudden flight.

"Hey, I just heard what happened! Everyone okay?" she asked.

Charm looked as beautiful as ever, always making Emma think of Snow White. Perfect creamy white skin and shiny black hair, while Emma had the unruly red hair, sprinkle of freckles and the green eyes of a pixie. *Double sigh.*

"Sort of." Emma hedged her bets with a fake grin. "Timmy shot Stone with Cupid's arrow."

"What? No!" Charm's expression scared Emma right down to her running shoes. She shivered as a trickle of dread crawled its way down her spine. She'd been warned that this might not be a good thing. She needed more facts and she needed them yesterday.

"Yup, got him right in the—" Ace was interrupted by Emma, who accidently stepped on his instep.

"Ow, what was that for?" he demanded.

"Sorry, my foot slipped." She gave a fake look of sympathy and leaned in closer to whisper, certain he was going to say the exact wrong word that any red-blooded male would say about his brother. "Did you know that Granny Toogood is within listening range?" Charm's grandmother was a stickler for not swearing and she'd just joined the small crowd on the sidewalk.

Emma moved back, adding, "I gotta go. Take Timmy back to his mother." She looked around but couldn't see Vanity anywhere in sight. Natch.

"Yeah, sure." Charm was kept busy chewing on a thumbnail, looking decidedly perturbed.

"I'll come with," Stone volunteered.

It was on the tip of her tongue to ask why, since he didn't know her or Timmy's mother from shinola, but she held it in. Maybe a few dozen chocolates would help ease the situation anyway. Some laced with caffeine would be perfect. Or a soothing liqueur.

"Me too," Ace said.

"Me three," Charm said.

"Okay." *Well, this is just weird.*

And so, the troop marched its way through the crowd that was breaking up now that the best part of the shenanigans was concluded—hopefully for the day—and down the street to her new candy shop.

Emma had a bad feeling, though, that it was really only the conclusion of Act One, and not the entire play.

"Chocolate, anyone?" she asked, picking up an opened box from the counter and holding it out. Vanity stepped up first and nabbed a few, handing a couple to Timmy, who just couldn't seem to get enough sugar into his system.

"Thanks, we'll be off now."

"Are you sure there isn't anything you want to buy?" Emma asked pointedly. The woman was notorious for allowing her son to graze, then stepping away from the scene of the crime. And while Emma hadn't said much of anything about it to date, today she felt owed. Emma had taken the hit for her son's behavior, certain that Stone still believed she was the one who had shot him. The woman blushed and pointed at the chocolate truffle display.

"I'll take three of them." When she saw that Emma was going for a paper sack, the less expensive option for so few chocolates, she added, "in a box, if you please."

Emma did as she was bidden, took her exact handful of change, then watched the woman leave, her son trailing her and still eyeing the bow that she'd placed on the top shelf behind the counter. She squinted her eyes at him. *Just you try, young man.*

Home of Erotic Romance

Sign up for our newsletter and find out about all our romance book releases, eBook sales and promotions, sneak peeks and FREE romance books!

About the Author

A loyal Chicago girl who loves deep dish pizza, the Cubs, and The Lake, her close fam moved to TN so she ends up visiting the South more than she ever planned! CC Dragon is fascinated by the magical and paranormal as well as the quirks of the south. She loves creating characters who solve mysteries. A coffee and chocolate addict who loves fast cars, she's still looking for a hero who likes to cook and clean…so she can write more!

CC Dragon loves to hear from readers. You can find her contact information, website details and author profile page at https://www.totallybound.com

www.ingramcontent.com/pod-product-compliance
Lightning Source LLC
Chambersburg PA
CBHW031912190626
46814CB00003BA/871